MW00767928

JONATHAN STURAK

# GEEK vs VEGAS

A NOVEL

ALSO BY JONATHAN STURAK

NOVELS

*HIS FIRST, HER LAST*

*VEGAS WAS HER NAME*

*A SMUDGE OF GRAY*

*CLOUDED RAINBOW*

COLLECTIONS

*FROM VEGAS WITH BLOOD*

STORIES

*FEED ME*

PENDAN PUBLISHING

*Copyright © 2014 by Jonathan Sturak.*

*All rights reserved.*

Published in the United States of America by
Pendan Publishing

This is a work of fiction. All names, characters, organizations, places, events, and incidents are used fictitiously and/or are products of the author's imagination. Any resemblance to actual persons, living or dead, events, or locales is purely coincidental.

The Library of Congress has catalogued the paperback edition as follows:
Sturak, Jonathan
Geek vs Vegas / by Jonathan Sturak
p. cm.
ISBN: 978-0-9825-8945-8

www.sturak.com

*For R.S.*

# GEEK vs VEGAS

# 1

Think about your significant other—your boyfriend, your girlfriend, your spouse. What do you do when you see them? Kiss them, right? It's like clockwork. You lower or raise your head, depending on your height, angle your chin correctly, and then lay one on him or her. Significant others are easy. If I had a girlfriend, I would kiss her until she told me to stop.

Etiquette with coworkers, however, is a different story. Men are okay. I shake hands with Steve from Finance or Greg from Billing. It's easy. However, women are problematic. What are you supposed to do? An introduction is usually simple—a handshake. Then it only gets more awkward from there. What should you do when your female coworker is leaving on a long vacation, or she announces she's having a baby, or she just lost a loved one and it's her first day back, or it's that moment just after you exchange gifts with her at the holiday party?

One time, Betty from the Help Desk gave me a Christmas card as she was leaving for the day. There was no one else around. I stood up from my seat to accept it. I figured that much out on my own, but when she handed it to me, her bug eyes—you know, those eyes that look like toy eyes on springs—suggested she wanted something else. She leaned in after I had already gone for the shake, so I had no choice but to hug her. Then I didn't know what to do about the peck on the cheek. I left it at the hug, and so did she. Come to think of it, I never even read that card.

Is the peck on the cheek okay at work? Or is it only okay in Europe? If you think about it, it's usually not the actual peck that matters, the lips-on-cheek contact, but rather the implied peck, the sound of the pucker and release in the ear of the person you're hugging. If you make the sound and the other person doesn't, you risk crossing the line, a sexual harassment cry, but if you don't make the sound and the other person does, you look like a coldhearted coworker—one with no potential for promotion. The secret is timing, reading the signals, studying the body language to go with the flow. A geek does not possess these things.

My mind is wandering because I'm at a urinal, standing alone inside the men's room at Pegman Telecommunications in Los Angeles. As I'm here and unable to pee, I hear the door open. Urinal etiquette requires eyes forward, no sudden movements. The sound of exhaling is okay, but definitely not the sound of farting. I must look forward at this crack in the white tile. It's a big crack. Who made this crack? I don't hear the clomp of a pair of dress shoes. Dress shoes are required attire here, a part of the business professional dress code.

I still can't pee, but I give in. I glance to my side and see only my short-sleeve white dress shirt and polka dot tie in the mirror. Who opened the door? Wait. There's a dog behind me. It's a big dog, like the one in that show *Lassie*. However, the longer I look at it, the more I realize that this dog is not like the one I remember from the show. It growls at me, showing its teeth. I clutch my penis.

The door opens again. It's my boss, Ms. Dipple! "There you are, Rusty," she says.

The dog trots to her side.

I stare at the crack. There's no way I can pee now, even though my bladder is ready to explode.

"Oh, Benjamin. I hope Mr. Pegman's pooch didn't scare ya," she continues.

"Uh, I'm trying to use the bathroom here, Ms. Dipple," I say.

"Well, when you get to be CEO of your own company, you can have a private bathroom."

"But this is the men's room."

This woman is Goliath and I am David. She is Frankenstein and I am that little girl he drowned, or maybe that should be the other way around. When I started this job three years ago, I had a boss named Bruce, an Ohio State graduate ten years my senior. He was a cool guy with a cool collection of burned movies from Netflix. Every disc he got in the mail, he would burn and put in a binder. He would brag about how many discs he had. Then one day he was gone. They said he moved back to Ohio, but I think the movie industry got him. Regardless of what happened to Bruce, Ms. Dipple replaced him. How did she become the Director of Information Technology? She reminds me of the fifty-year-old lady at Wal-Mart who greets you at the door with that high-pitched voice and creepy smirk. I have to deal with this every day of the week, and even on weekends when Ms. Dipple includes me on a conference call with the Help Desk. Thank God I can hide behind the phone.

"What was that, Benjamin?" Ms. Dipple chuckles as she steals my manhood. "*Anywho*. I hope you didn't forget about the presentation at three o'clock. Very important, mister."

"Well, if I can finish in the bathroom, I might be able to finish the slides."

"You have one hour. Watch your zipper on its way up," she says, adding another nasally laugh. The dog scratches at the door. "Oh, you silly boy. Let's get you back to your daddy."

Ms. Dipple and Cujo leave the bathroom, and leave me in peace. Now I can finish urinating. Finally, some silence. I stare at the crack in the tile, hearing the void of nothingness—no copiers, no computers, no coworkers. Yet I still can't pee! It's as if Ms. Dipple has corked my bladder. Come on! Piss already!

I whistle as if I'm a six-year-old back in Pennsylvania, my mom waiting to use the bathroom. Finally, a stream starts. I exhale…but then the door opens again, causing me to stop. Not again!

This time, I hear people talking; at least they're men! It's Gary and Charlie from Sales. These guys are like my obnoxious uncles at Christmas; you know, the ones who always drill you about your life, your ambitions, your love life. You never see these relatives until the holidays, then they want a year-end review right on the spot, and they do it right in front of everyone, including grandma!

Both of them slide next to me—no buffer zone of one urinal, no quiet time to say your prayers. I'm sandwiched between my two uncles!

"Franklin has a horrible sports program. We had our nine-year-old in there for a year, but then we went private and enrolled him in Shady Maple. Some big name swimmers were alumni there," Gary goes.

"If we buy that condo like we planned, we'll be in Franklin's zone," Charlie says.

Why do some men talk when they are doing their business? I need to concentrate, to start the stream in silence, to make sure I get it all out. I'm trying to prevent a urinary tract infection here, but other men, like Gary with the beer gut and Charlie with the gray hair, treat this like a board meeting. Come on! I have to finish before them. Urinals are queues—first in, first out. If these guys finish before me, they'll think I have a problem; they might tell the office!

"Well, enroll him in Shady Maple. The money's well worth it," Gary continues.

I can see his stream in the corner of my eye. Why did I just look?!

"Hey, Bill Gates, how's it hanging?" Charlie says, catching my glance.

"It's Benjamin," I reply.

"Benjamin Gates then."

"I hear you're giving us a briefing today at three. Can't wait," Gary says.

"Mary from Accounting is going to be there," Charlie responds for me.

"She's got a perfect rack. Don't you think, Benjamin?" Gary goes.

I think about Mary's sun-spotted skin as my penis is in my hand. Oh my God…yuck! "She's nearly as old as my mom."

I'm done. I can't pee. It's useless. Maybe I should go into the women's room. I shake it, and grab the zipper. "Watch your zipper on its way up," Ms. Dipple says inside my head.

The water in the urinal is still clear, a perfect drink for a dog.

"When you get to be our age, a woman in her forties is golden. You'll see," Gary says.

In the mirror, I look through my thick glasses and into my green eyes, but I see those two humping the urinals. I take off my I.D. badge from around my neck and start to wash.

"How old are you?" Charlie asks.

"Twenty-six," I reply.

"Ha! I have golf clubs older than you," Charlie says.

I need to get the hell out of here. I take two towels and wipe. Each guy hits the flush at the same time. Who are these guys? Do they coordinate eating too? They should have flushed each other's urinal to make it all romantic.

"See ya at three, guys," I say, making a break for the door.

I smile, realizing who these two guys remind me of—two old college roommates.

# 2

My title is Information Systems Policy Analyst. My job is a desk jockey. I write and implement computer policies to prevent people from downloading porn, and then I fix their computers from malware after they figure out how to download porn anyway. This is 95% of my job with the other 5% being "other duties as assigned." One time, I had to fix the vending machine in the break room. Ms. Dipple's Doritos were stuck.

Pegman Telecommunications is comprised of about one hundred onsite employees here in Los Angeles, with service people roaming the streets. What we do is simple—sell television service to gullible people in LA. Pretend Comcast, Cox, DirecTV, and Dish Network all have giant castles with guards, moats, and dragons. Then there is Pegman Telecom knocking on their castle gates, trying to steal their peasants away.

We offer these bizarre packages, the twenty-four hour reality channels, the *Latin Lust* network, non-stop '80s men's action movies, and more gay and lesbian channels than an old retired couple could know what to do with. We'll be out of business before I start losing my hair. The pay is $40,000 a year, which sounds like a fortune when you get the job offer living in the snowy mountains in Pennsylvania, but it's poverty level when you walk out of LAX and see the taxi rates.

I've been working at this job for three years now. I don't have any friends. I don't own a refrigerator. I do own a car, which required me to sign my life away. I don't know why I moved out to LA after college. I thought I'd be working as a Hollywood special-effects wizard cruising Sunset Boulevard with a blonde—no, a redhead—next to me. But that hasn't happened, not even close, and I'm about ready to go back to Pennsylvania, back to the snowy mountains, back to the gloom, back to the uncles who drill me at Christmas—nah, maybe I'll stay here just a little longer.

As I leave the bathroom, I walk through our hallways and see maintenance men installing new keycard locks on the doors. We got our new badges already; they were passed out last week. In two days, these will be our keys to move in and out of the doorways on the floor. Just to go from the bathroom to my desk, I will need to swipe three times. The big boss wants this place locked down. He thinks the credit card numbers of the customers are a hot target ever since he caught a man off the street in our break room snooping around. The boss sent out a nasty email about this, which was leaked to our competitors. To assure the customers that their personal information is secure, the boss launched a full-scale investigation. It turned out that the burglar in the break room was a homeless guy looking for leftovers. That's when the big boss tasked Ms. Dipple to implement a physical security system, which then landed on my desk. I designed the policy—that's what the big meeting is all about at 3:00 today, my time to shine.

I pass Rowena, our office assistant to the big boss. She has eyes like a cat and can spot you from a mile away. She probably saw me in the bathroom.

"You got the conference room at three," she says as I pass by.

"The highlight of my day," I mutter.

I walk onto the main floor. There are more cubicles here than at the warehouse of the company that makes cubicles. It's as if we're rats looking for the cheese in our maze.

When I reference the departments, I really mean different sections of the floor. When it all comes down to it, we're all just really one and the same.

I near a cubicle of a guy I never met. He must work here because he's always in this cubicle, but no one ever talks to him, and he never talks to anyone. What is that smell? Is that fungus? The guy is cutting his toenails in his cubicle. I need to find another way to my desk. This is just getting weird!

Around the corner, someone's clanking on a keyboard. It's Regina, the former hooker, now a grandmother and a secretary. She still wears makeup as if it's a day of reprieve for the Amish.

"There's the *cutie patootie*," she says.

I can see her reflection in the fisheye mirror on top of her monitor. I should get one of those.

"Come here, you. Computer question," she continues.

She got me.

"I have this Microsoft Word document. How do I have the page numbers only start showing on page two?" she asks.

"May I?" I ask as I hover over her and go to grab the mouse.

"You can touch my computer any time, you little devil."

I get her innuendo, but before I swallow it, the smell of her perfume swallows me. It smells like a burning rose mixed with a skunk. In her Word doc, I click the Page Number button on the Insert Ribbon, and then insert page numbers centered in the footer, ensuring to select "Different First Page" on the advanced options. There it is.

"All those click, click, click, clicks. You have to sit down and show me sometime."

"It's all in the wrist," I say, scurrying away.

I turn one more corner and see an empty cubicle. My desk is across from it. This is my home away from home, my workbench, my locker room, my cafeteria, my life. A 19" CRT monitor sits on top of my desk. You know, one of those big boxes that weighs a hundred pounds. It's a dinosaur. Maybe this is why my glasses are so thick. The monitor is attached to a Dell computer running Windows XP. It's weak, but at least it's not the weakest computer in the building. We give those to the sales guys. They are the worst for looking up porn. Their excuses are that they were researching new clients, trying to find the demographic who watches the *Latin Lust* network. The slow computers keep them at bay.

Papers are stacked on the sides of my desk. Paper is great for soundproofing, so that's why I stack policy handbooks, security manuals, Microsoft Security Bulletins, and Internet usage reports all around me. The only piece of paper that I care to look at is the 8"x10" printout of my alma mater—Penn State University. The color blue and the Nittany Lion keep me mollified.

I take a seat and see an envelope on my desk—the mail boy must have been by when I went to the bathroom. Man, I have to piss. I should just piss in this empty water bottle and give it to Ms. Dipple. I'll tell her it's an energy drink.

Inside the envelope is my car loan statement. You miss one payment and they track you down, send you notices everywhere you were last seen, and put you in the Rolodex of all the collection agencies in town.

I check the clock: "2:18." There're forty-two minutes left until the big meeting, so I'd better finish this. Waking up my computer, I open the PowerPoint file labeled, "Information Systems Policy Update." I can't afford any more distractions.

"Hey, Benny, got you something," a male voice says.

It's Bob from over the cubicle wall. Bob's the older brother you never knew you had, the one who borrows your pen and doesn't return it, the one who invites you to lunch and makes you drive, the one you share whispers with about every employee. Bob has been here ever since I started. He's a big guy, easily a hundred pounds heavier than I am. He loves his desk, arrives at work before me, and leaves after. I respect Bob, because he knows how to defrag a hard drive in less than thirty seconds. He's a Systems Analyst, which means he is tied to his desk even more than I am. Bob prepares all the Internet usage reports; he's the Internet Nazi. Bob's position falls under Ms. Dipple. In fact, I was hoping the big boss would have promoted Bob to her job when Bruce left.

"Hey, Benny, you there? I got you something," Bob repeats.

I peer over the cubicle. There are Butterfinger wrappers scattering across his desk.

"What? A new job?" I respond.

"My afternoon snack. I picked you up something."

Bob opens his desk drawer and roots around. The buttons on his blue shirt are bulging. He has sweat stains radiating from his armpits. Come on, Bob. You're a mess.

He pulls out three McDonald's hamburgers, and then hands me a Happy Meal. Getting a Happy Meal from a grown man who is not your father is illegal in some states. Inside are fries, a hamburger, and a race car. I take the toy out and place it next to four other cars on top of my monitor. This should complete the collection.

"Great. Just what I needed. But the burger will hit the spot. I'll need the fuel for my presentation."

"Oh, that's right. You're on to brief the directors with the updated badge policy," he says, taking his badge off from around his neck. "Hey, where's yours?" Bob stands up. Bob never stands up.

I look down and see the polka dots on my tie glaring at me. "Oh shit!"

Where did I leave my badge? I look at the maze of cubicles. It could be anywhere!

"Missing something there, Benjamin?" a voice says from behind. It's Gary, holding my badge.

"Oh, thank you, sir," I say. I think this is the first time I called Gary *sir*. This is the guy who Googled, "Shemales Gone Wild."

"I found it the bathroom. I won't tell your boss about this one."

I noose my neck with the badge.

As Gary walks off, I make sure it's really my badge. There I am, Benjamin Pollock, Information Systems Policy Analyst, Pegman Telecommunications.

"You'll never guess what I saw in the bathroom," I say to Bob.

"You found your pubes?"

"I found them in the women's room," I reply.

"Nice come back, Benny."

"No. I saw a dog."

"This isn't some weird animal thing, is it?" Bob says.

"I'm serious. I was just standing there against the urinal, and then this big dog came in the bathroom. Then, Ms. Dipple walked in. She crossed the line."

"Wait. Hold on a second. So a dog, Ms. Dipple, and you were all in the bathroom?" Bob goes.

"Yeah."

"I should've filmed it so I could put it up on our website under the *About Us* tab."

I shake my head. If I had an electric razor, I'd slice the top of Bob's hair off when he sits back down. "Hey, Bob. What did you hear about *that*?" I gesture to the empty cubicle across from me.

"Not sure. Heard Ms. Dipple interviewed some, but nothing definite."

"I wonder if Natalie Portman is one of them," I say.

"Natalie Portman as a policy analyst?"

A man can dream, right? A new employee is like having a new student entering the class midyear; he's innocent until proven guilty. Is he a friend or a foe? A new employee always sides with the boss; after all, the boss just hired him. You can't just start badmouthing the boss to the new employee, because he will surely go tell the boss that he doesn't like his coworkers, meaning you!

"Did you know Natalie Portman and I were born in the same year?" I say.

"Stop dreaming, man," Bob says.

"Chop! Chop! Boys!" Ms. Dipple barks. She's holding papers. I hope they're not for me. "Three o'clock, Benjamin. Get going."

"Yes, ma'am," I say.

Bob and I sit back down. One time, Bob and I were debating who was hotter, Ashlee or Jessica Simpson. Bob said he liked blondes, so he voted for Jessica. I told him that I did too, but the touch of punk in Ashlee scored my vote, but then she got her nose job, and I lost interest.

Ms. Dipple is still over my shoulder. "Did either of you see Rusty? He's around here somewhere."

"Benjamin said he saw him in the men's room," Bob replies.

"That silly dog," she says, wandering away.

"You were right, Benny. Ms. Dipple is insane. Hey, one question. What's the function for standard deviation in Excel?"

"Uh, S.T.D.E.V. and the cells."

"Thanks!"

The hamburger from the Happy Meal is still hot. How does Bob even get his McDonald's in here? Ah, who cares? Bob's a good guy. I scroll to the last slide in my PowerPoint file. Only thirty-five minutes are left. A warm hamburger in my belly should speed this up. I reach for the unwrapped burger, but it's gone. I spin my chair and see that damn dog clutching my hamburger between its teeth. As I reach for it, the dog growls. It swallows the meal in two bites, and then trots away. I turn back to my screen, my stomach growling, my bladder screaming. I create a new slide on my 20" screen and start typing, "Cell Phone Use During Work Hours."

# 3

"Cell Phone Use During Work Hours" projects onto an 80" screen. I'm standing next to the screen and next to General Schwarzkopf during the Persian Gulf War, I mean Ms. Dipple. I relieved myself in the bathroom five minutes ago, no distractions this time; I locked myself in a stall.

This is our war room, the place where decisions are made and people are fired. I've been in this room a hundred times, but I never had an audience. I stand in front of at least twenty people seated around the conference table. They say to picture the people in your audience with their clothes off to make it go easier, but these people are all over forty and don't even take their clothes off at the beach. I'd rather picture them wearing suits of armor. Back at Penn State, I nearly failed my public speaking class, only getting a B minus because I fixed the professor's office computer.

There is Ms. Dipple, my boss, my Wal-Mart greeter. She had introduced me to this crowd, the directors of each department. She has the spotlight now, babbling about the increase in Internet traffic. No one is looking at me right now, but I'm looking at these robots.

Sleeping in the back is a guy with white hair, a handlebar mustache, and a corduroy suit. A buxom Polish lady from the Help Desk is sitting between Gary and Charlie. I do admit that she is not bad looking for an older woman, if you can understand her words. Who hires a woman with a thick Eastern European accent to man the phones at the Help Desk? I bet our customers think we're trying to sell communist propaganda packages.

Maybe I should date an older woman. I've never dated anyone older than me, but then again, I haven't dated anyone regularly since college. Besides, those college girls just used me to do their math homework. The last date I had was with the niece of Bob's sister. Why wasn't she simply Bob's niece? I still haven't figured that one out. The girl looked like one of those professional wrestlers—not a hot female one with a ripped body, more like a 300-pound fat man drenched in sweat. We only went on one date, and then I had to delouse my car.

Ms. Dipple is done ranting, and so am I.

"Who here has a personal cell phone?" I say to my captive audience.

Everyone raises his or her hand, including the sleeping mustache man. So he *is* listening.

"Does anyone know the policy regarding its usage during business hours?" I continue.

I click to the next slide: "Personal Cell Phone Use Is Prohibited Except During Designated Breaks."

"Tell that one to my wife," Charlie says.

The only one who laughs is Gary. Ms. Dipple glares at him. Gary and Charlie shut up. So they're scared of her too.

I go to the next slide: "Workstation Policy – Do Not Shut Down Workstation."

"As a reminder, ensure you leave your PC on before you leave for the day," I say.

Gary sits up. "Should we restart or log off before we leave?"

"Either or. Just don't shut down."

"Well, which is it. Restart or log off?" Charlie adds.

I guess these guys are mad that Mary from Accounting couldn't make it. I want to say, "Stop downloading monkey porn." Instead, I say, "I would recommend a restart. That way, the machine gets a fresh boot and stays at the login prompt. But again, do not shut down."

The Polish lady says, "I want the power to dominate global economy."

Mustache man wakes up as everyone looks at her. Did she just make a communist slur? Mustache man translates, "She said—all that power waste contributes to global warming."

We all exhale.

"Here goes the feminist liberal talk," Gary says.

Charlie chuckles.

"I plot to blow up the government," she says.

Did she just say that?

"She said—at least I care about the environment," mustache man translates.

"I'm only the messenger, ma'am. This has been vetted through my department. The desktop administrators send updates to the systems at night, so the computers need to stay on twenty-four seven."

Ms. Dipple gives me a wink and a nod.

The room dies down, so I click to the next slide. A copy of my badge displays in 50 inches of glory. Laughter hits me. These bastards! If I find out who's laughing, I'll smother them with toner.

I turn and see everyone laughing. "And the newest policy is with your new I.D. badges. As you know, we recently had a break-in. We need to lock this place down like the Department of Defense."

"So, are we all spies now?" Charlie asks.

"The powers that run this place require us to issue new badges that contain proximity chips to allow entry in and out of the building. Mr. Pegman has expressed his strong compliance with this policy. Improper handling of your badge will be grounds for civil and criminal offenses and public humility… Mr. Pegman's words, not mine… And of course, you will lose your job. Therefore, our new policy is…"

On the next screen, in bold Times New Roman 120 point font, I read aloud, "Lose your badge, your job loses you."

"That sounds a bit harsh," Gary says.

"Here goes the lawless conservative talk," the Polish lady says.

Everyone looks at mustache man. "That's what she said."

"It's the new policy coming straight from the front office," I continue.

Suddenly, Michael Jackson's "Beat It" fills the room, bouncing off the posters for *Latin Lust* and *The Monster Channel*. Everyone looks around. The only person in the room who knows where it's coming from is me.

I reach into my pocket and press buttons on my cell phone, but it won't silence! I remove it and see that the caller ID reads, "Unknown." I find the ignore button, silencing the phone. My face flushes. Oops.

"Ahh, someone's losing their job," Charlie says.

"You write 'em, but you don't follow 'em," Gary says.

I think the best thing to do is to do nothing. That's what my grandmother used to say, my dad's mom.

"Are there any questions?" I ask.

# 4

I'm walking back to my desk. It feels cool in here, especially around my crotch. Oh shit! My zipper is down. Was it down when I gave the presentation? Was that why Ms. Dipple was winking at me?

I zip up, the sound of the motion louder than expected.

"I heard that, you silly *cutie patootie*," the ex-hooker says. How did she hear me? I guess it's all those years of unzipping her clients.

The smell of hamburgers hits me. Bob must be refueling before he leaves. I make it back to my desk and peer over the cubicle wall, but all I see is Bob's empty chair. Did he leave a burger?

"He had a doctor's appointment," Ms. Dipple says from behind me.

"That doesn't surprise me," I reply.

Ms. Dipple approaches and hits me with a chalky smell. Is that antifungal spray?

"Since Bob is not here, I have to ask you." Her voice lowers. "Do you think Bob has been pulling his weight?"

"Uh, what do you mean?"

"Well, we just want to make sure that everyone is being fully utilized. No freeloaders."

"Bob doesn't miss a website in his report. I think he's great. If anything, we need extra help with the software upgrades." I gesture to the empty desk.

"My lips are sealed on that," she says.

I swallow my tongue. Why did she ask me about Bob? Did she ask Bob about *me*? Is she going to fire me? This doesn't feel right.

"I just want to say that you did a great job in there, Benjamin. I found my new *briefer*." The way she opens her mouth when saying *briefer* sends a shiver down my spine. Did she see my briefs through my open zipper?

"Uh, thank you, Ms. Dipple."

"The cell phone trick was a nice touch. Show them what *not* to do. Well done," she says as she hands me some Starburst candy.

"And I don't even have to wear a costume," I say.

"Don't worry, Benjamin. If they let one of you go, I'll do my best to keep you."

"Very reassuring," I reply. Am I going to get fired? Shit!

"I need you to check the Ethernet cables in the front office and make sure they're all compliant with the update," she says.

"It's almost quitting time."

"This is the best time, since most have left for the day. Remember, Benjamin, there's no *I* in team, but there's an *I* in fired."

Ms. Dipple walks off. I'm sure she's heading to the door. I sit down at my desk. It's 4:13. I wish I could go. I'm craving an evening at Panera Bread. A "You Pick Two" combo with a half Asiago Roast Beef Sandwich, creamy tomato soup, a whole grain baguette, and my laptop. I could watch some episodes of *Seinfeld* while sipping my soup. I could go to that Panera on Wilshire. That waitress there, Emily, always laughs at my jokes. Or is it Emmy?

I wake up my computer, but my password doesn't work. I try a second time, and it still doesn't work. My password is the first three letters of my three aunts, with capitalizing the last one. My mom's sister is named Helen. Elizabeth and Suzanne are the names of my dad's sisters. So that makes *heleliSUZ* when you do the math. I crack my fingers, and try it one letter at a time. It finally works. Why is the third time always the charm?

I minimize the PowerPoint file and see the picture of Wonder Woman as my Windows desktop background. A girl in charge is what I'm looking for. Down in the system tray next to the clock is a little envelope. Let's see who emailed me.

Inside Microsoft Outlook, there's one new message. The sender is "Latin Lover 2000." I don't know a Latin Lover 2000. He must've sneaked his way through the spam filter. The subject says, "How To Tell You're At A Gay Bar." I grab the message and drag it over to the trash bin, but something stops me. I kinda wonder how I would know if I'm at a gay bar. That's important knowledge. I bet it shows a bunch of hairy guys with assless chaps dancing on a bar. That would be funny, but it's too obvious. Or maybe it shows a lit sign for a place called, "Gaylee's Bar," but the lights are burned out so that it only reads, "Gay Bar." Yeah, that would be a great pic.

I bring the message back and decide to live on the wild side. I open it up and see a picture of twenty men in dress shirts and ties all at a bar with a naked college girl standing front and center; not even one of the guys is looking at her.

I chuckle aloud. That's funny. Wow, this girl has nice boobs—looks about a B-cup. They are so perky. I like perky boobs, the ones with nipples looking you in the eye and not at your feet.

"Warning – Virus Detected In E-Mail" pops on the screen.

"Oh shit!" I shout.

"No cursing on the floor," Ms. Dipple says from over the wall.

I hammer the mouse and close the email, but the message still appears. Window after window with the same message pops up.

"Oh no. No... No..."

I push papers aside, drop to my knees, and yank the cord out. "Beat It" plays. I thought I put my phone on vibrate. Again, the phone shows, "Unknown." Who the hell is this? Is it Ms. Dipple firing me for getting a virus?

"Uh, hello," I answer.

"Is this Benjamin Pollock?" a deep voice asks.

"Who is this?"

"This is the police department. We have a warrant for your arrest."

My stomach twists. "What?! That's impossible!"

Did I do something illegal? I know I've been doing a rolling stop when I make a right turn on red. Who doesn't do that? But wait, the cops don't call to arrest you, but what if they did?

"You have many unpaid parking tickets," the voice continues.

"Unpaid parking tickets? No, you must be mistaken," I say instinctively. He must have the wrong guy.

"Ha! You really don't know who this is?" the voice says, changing tone.

Neurons fire and synapses surge. The voice is buried somewhere inside my brain. I recall the taste of a White Castle Hamburger, the image of Robert De Niro in *Ronin*, the high waist of my Computer Science professor. The voice reveals itself in the pile. It's Javier, my old college roommate at Penn State.

"Now I do, you jerk. Javier, how the hell are you?" I say.

"I'm sorry, man. I really had you going. I've been great."

Javier lived with me for my last two years of school. He's two years older than I am, but he was on the six-year college plan. Javier was a finance major who lived off his lawyer father, and was often seen roaming the streets of State College borrowing cigarettes and booze from freshman. Javier was my roommate, not by choice, but by chance. Penn State assigned him to share a fridge, a shower, the same air with me. Little did I know, Penn State married the brain with the brainless, the book smart with the panty smart. I remember the first time I met him. He was wearing a robe and had a glass of wine in his hand, and it was two o'clock in the afternoon. However, over time, Javier kept me sane, providing the comic relief, the drunken laughs, and the sobering cries. After graduating, I lost touch with Javier; we all seem to lose touch with friends after graduating.

I grab some yellow Ethernet cables from a box next to my desk and a Bluetooth headset for my phone from my desk drawer.

"So, how long's it been?" I say, even though I know the answer.

I walk into the front office for Mr. Pegman. There are three desks here, all abandoned by workers who have already called it a day.

"Three years," Javier says.

"I can't believe it's been three years."

I crawl under a desk and check the Ethernet cable. We are upgrading the front office to a Gigabit network. Only the secretaries to the president get the speed upgrade so they can balance the boss' checkbook faster, or so they say. It's really so they can brag to the others. These secretaries have their own rank system rivaling the military's. My job is to swap out the blue Cat 5e cables with the more robust Cat 6 cables. These will ensure reliability from the wall to the computers. As I'm under the desk, I find a raisin and two red Skittles.

"What are you doing, Benjamin? Are you masturbating?" Javier says.

"I'm still at work, just under a desk."

"You're under the secretary's desk, huh?"

"Actually, I am, but there's no secretary, just cables."

"Hey, I have a computer question," Javier says.

"So *this* is why you called."

A computer geek is an oxymoron. People bribe us for our computer skills. They offer us their lunches; they give us candy; they thank us till they're blue. Hot girls ask us for our brain all the time, but they never give us sex in exchange for our skills. You think it's easy being a computer geek, don't you? You think we know the answer to every computer question. You think it's easy for us and that we don't mind answering. Although we know a lot about computers, we don't know *every* answer. But we do know where to *find* the answer; that's what makes us who we are. We can use Google to find the answer to any computer question, and once we do, we store it inside our brains. We differ from the computer illiterate with the storage system of our brains, which can retrieve these answers quickly and accurately. Most people don't get it. They gladly give a barber ten bucks for a trim, an ice cream man a five for a single scoop of vanilla, and an escort a cool grand for an hour of her service. Why can't computer geeks be paid for their time? Enough favors! Treat us like male escorts—our time, our brain, is our money, just like a hooker's hands. Perhaps the real reason why people exploit computer geeks is that we are afraid to say *no*. We lack the social skills that the burly barber, the over-worked ice cream man, and the lethal escort have. We build up our tension, our anger, our rage, and then go postal…or write a book.

"You know everything about computers, but I want to catch up too," Javier says.

And computer geeks fall for flattery.

"Hey, my computer keeps locking after I boot it up. What can I do?" he asks.

"Could be anything. It's probably all that porn on there," I say as I crawl under the second desk and change the cable.

"Hmm, porn, right. So, you still living in PA?"

"No, Los Angeles."

"Damn. Really? Glad you kept your same number since Penn State."

"I have more friends back in PA than I do here."

"So you finally moved out there. I remember you talking about it back in college."

"I said a lot of things back then. You still working in Philly?"

"Nah, man, I moved to Vegas last year."

"Damn! Vegas?" I exclaim.

I've never been to Las Vegas, the proverbial Sin City, the oasis they glamorize in movies, the place with the warnings and catchphrases. I flew over Vegas on my way to LA, but from the plane, it looked like a grain of sand on the beach. But that grain of sand is filled with sex, gambling, booze, and heat—a perfect place for Javier.

"It's kickin'," Javier says. "I got my own bachelor pad and working as a club promoter. I'm brushing shoulders with the big dogs."

I go under the third desk and see the dog sleeping. There's a blue cable behind the mongrel. Should I change it? They always say to let sleeping dogs lie. Hmm. I stand up and glance at the ominous door with the words *Mr. Pegman – President* written in Arial font. Hmm. Should I check the boss' cable? Surely, he will be getting the faster network.

I open the door and see a mahogany bookcase, a leather couch, *The Starry Night* on the wall, and a desk long enough to land a small plane. I also see Mr. Pegman and a woman in a business suit kissing on top of the desk as if there's no tomorrow. I pull the door shut as quietly as I can before they see me. Luckily, his office is huge. This could've been very bad. Whew!

"What was that?" Javier asks.

"I just walked into a lion's den."

"Lion's den? Are you working computer effects for Spielberg?" he asks.

"No."

"Lucas?"

"No. Dipple."

"Is he European?"

"I'm pushing papers at the moment. Still waiting on Spielberg's call," I say.

"Pushing papers? Sounds deadly."

"Hey, I just bought a car so I need this job. Things are tight."

The dog gets up and looks at me. I show it the cables in my hand; it seems to work. The dog walks away. I drop down and swap the blue for the yellow. I'm quick with this one.

"You got a girl out there?" Javier asks as I kneel to stand up.

There's a barrage of photographs on the top of the desk. There I am in one from last year's holiday party. I'm in the middle of a conga line surrounded by an army of Pegman Telecommunications' finest women in their fifties and sixties.

"Girl? Well, I have plenty of Bingo partners to choose from. Life pretty much sucks right now."

I'm finished so I head back to my desk.

"You should come out to Vegas. Let's party like we used to," Javier says.

"Like *we* used to? Remember, Javier. You partied. I watched. You just want me to fix your computer."

"Well, I do need to get on there and pay some bills. So what do you say?" he presses.

I make it back to my desk and dump the cables. "I have some vacation time coming up."

"No. Tonight," he says with a deep voice, the same voice he used to prank me when he called.

"Tonight? I have to work tomorrow."

I don't tell him that I crave to go to Panera tonight; some creamy tomato soup would be sobering after seeing inside the lion's den. I take him off Bluetooth.

"Take a sick day tomorrow. It's a four-hour drive. We'll pull an all-nighter like back in the dorms. Instead of books and paper, it'll be tits and ass."

As I stare at the Penn State poster tacked to my cubicle wall, my eyes shift from the face of the Nittany Lion to the face of another lion—Ms. Dipple.

"Hold on," I say into the phone.

"Are you on the phone, Benjamin? Who is that?" Ms. Dipple says.

"It's my mother in PA. She's, uh, having a baby," I lie.

"Your mother's pregnant? How old is she?"

"No, I mean my sister."

"Well, you know the policy," she says.

I hate these policies. Who designed them? Oh, yeah… I did. "I know, Ms. Dipple, but this is a family emergency."

"Make it snappy. Are you done with the cables?" she asks.

“The only one I didn’t get was Mr. Pegman’s office. I didn’t know if his computer is getting the upgrade.”

“Oh, I forgot to tell you. He’s having an important meeting with an auditor. You can get it in the morning. By the way, I have a card for you to sign. It’s Kate’s birthday in Finance. She’s going to be sixty.”

“That’s great, but I don’t know her,” I say.

Ms. Dipple widens her eyes and molests me with her glare, the wrinkle between her eyes forming the shape of an angry vagina. She lays the card on my desk. “Sign it!” she yaps, and then walks away.

I only saw that look on her face once before when she forced me to go to the holiday party. She said I had to be there in case the DJ’s equipment broke. His equipment didn’t break, but I wish it did. Instead, I got center stage in the conga line.

Oh, I forgot about Javier. “Hey, I’m back,” I say into the phone.

“Who the hell was that?” he asks.

“My boss.”

“Sounds like she’s from the Third Reich. Anyway, you need one night to let go, man. Sounds like you need to get laid.”

Ahh, getting laid. I can’t even remember what it’s like to get laid. Since living in LA for three years, I’ve had no college girls, no ladies, no drunken girls with beer goggles, no cougars satisfying a fantasy of a younger man, no coworkers (yuck!), not even a hooker. I did get a hand job at this massage parlor in West Hollywood. Honestly, I was just looking for a massage to fix my back from the chair I used to have at work, which lacked lumbar support. The Asian masseuse took charge. When I was face down, she got up on the table and walked on my back. I was too sore to say no to the hand job. She could've been pulling on my big toe for all that I knew because I lost all feeling below the waist after she pummeled me. The girls that I had in my past, all three of them, had the same look of evil that Ms. Dipple just shared with me. These three encounters were more like conjugal visits than *real* sexual encounters. The moment I got each of their clothes off, I was in for a surprise. I had one whisper that she was recovering from meningitis. The second one said that she was raped the night before, and the last one was drop dead gorgeous, a blonde with big lips, until I found her penis. Once her, rather *his*, pants came off, I was out the door and crying in the shower. Ahh, college life. I miss those days. Come to think of it, Javier set me up with those two and a half ladies. Maybe that's why I haven't been laid since college.

"I need to get laid? Don't tell me you're hitting for the other team now," I say to Javier.

"No! I'm talking about a Vegas vixen. One of these chicks out here will renew your engine for another thirty thousand."

"Sounds tempting," I say. Two little Benjamins are on my shoulders. One is dressed in a Hugo Boss pinstriped suit with his hair slicked back and with a glass of wine in his hand. The other is wearing a white shirt with a polka dot tie holding Ethernet cables. Wait, that's actually me right now.

"So, you down?" Javier says.

Now a woman in a red dress is caressing the pinstripes on Vegas Benjamin and Ms. Dipple is rubbing her claws on LA Benjamin. Which one is it going to be?

"Vegas vixen, huh?" I say.

I've never done anything like this since moving to Los Angeles. I shower every night at nine, watch reruns of *Cheers* until eleven, and then dream about exotic women until my alarm blares at seven. With this offer, I won't have to dream about exotic women tonight; I can be with them, right next to them. Oh, that would be nice. Javier used to give me the crazy college girls, but now he can give me a crazy Vegas girl. I like crazy Vegas girls.

# 5

It's 5:05 and I'm in the parking garage inside my Scion xB. It's a compact car, fits *one* uncomfortably. If SpongeBob had a car, he would have a Scion. I'm thinking about Javier, about my drive, about the Vegas girls. This is what I need. Javier is right.

I pull out of my space, but a sedan cuts me off and sends me screeching to a halt. It's Ms. Dipple!

"I just can't get rid of you."

I follow her down the aisle, slowly, steadily. She's driving a white Chevy Impala covered in dust. Where did she drive that thing? There's a bumper sticker on her car: "Party Girl." You've got to be kidding me. Really, Ms. Dipple?

She pulls out slower than a car at the exit to a bingo parlor. Finally, she makes her turn. I speed around her and glance. There's Ms. Dipple hunkered down in the seat, hands gripping the wheel, oblivious to me next to her. To see your boss in the outside world changes things. No longer can she tell you to fix her computer, to install cables, to sign a card. As I race to the intersection, to freedom, the light turns red. I have to stop, and there is Ms. Dipple right next to me.

After you say goodbye to a person, drive away, and then see her at the next traffic light, there are two choices. Either you acknowledge her by smiling and waving—a continuation of your meeting—or you let her keep driving as if she is a stranger. Do you say *goodbye* a second time, or after you've said it once, that's it? In my situation, I hope for the latter, but Ms. Dipple chooses the former. She looks over, rolls down the window, and signals for me to do the same. I give in.

"Hi, Benjamin. Don't forget your badge," she says with her silly smile.

"I have it right here," I reply, holding it up.

"Let me cut in front of you. I have to turn left up there. I forgot that I have to get my hair done."

The light turns green and I let her over. I guess she is still in charge.

Los Angeles traffic is like bits of data traveling through the motherboard in a computer. There are freeways, bridges, gaps, one-ways, detours, and alternate routes. Looking at it from the sky is like looking inside the case of a computer. The only problem is that you're a tiny little bit, traversing the computer, and computers don't need every bit to reach its destination. That's why they invented error correction, so that if one bit fails to reach its destination, the computer will still work. I am that bit, and I hope I make it to my destination.

As I creep along the freeway during rush hour, I listen to classical music—Beethoven's "Moonlight Sonata," a hypnotic tune that pacifies me, keeps me sane inside when there's insanity outside. I don't exactly know where I am going, just the direction of east. However, as I make it through West Covina on the 10 freeway, I get a text with the directions from the man leading me into the unknown. I don't know what to expect when I get to my final destination, but I'm feeling alive; this is going to be the night of Benjamin.

About an hour later, I finally hit the 15. Traffic is flowing and I'm listening to some Smashing Pumpkins, the guitar-cranking "Bullet with Butterfly Wings." Life is great.

After another hour, the sun says goodbye behind me. Gone are the concrete pillars, buildings, homes—Los Angeles. I'm on a four-lane highway with nothing but brown around me. Smooth jazz is flowing through my ears. I like smooth jazz when I'm feeling nervous. It reminds me of watching The Weather Channel, the *Local on the 8s*. It reminds me of my dad, who would watch The Weather Channel as my mom would watch the Home Shopping Network. I should call my parents, but the signal of my phone is lost, the screen reading, "Searching for service..." Where am I going? I'm hungry. There's a sign for Barstow. I'm going to stop. I glance in the rear-view mirror; this might be the last time I ever see the sun.

It's now night and I'm chowing down on a hamburger from the drive-thru at In-N-Out Burger. I didn't even get out of the car. I have now crossed the halfway point, the point of no return. It's now longer to go back than to finish. I switch the radio to some opera music. Listening to a large woman screaming at me reminds me of Ms. Dipple at work; it reminds me of my life.

After another hour, I cross into the state of Nevada. There's nothing—only the void of the desert around me. The headlights that are flowing in a line look like the last pathway to the Central Processing Unit.

I decide to follow a teal Toyota minivan when the opera station gets lost. Now I only get classic rock. I'm listening to The Doors' "Love Her Madly." It's an uplifting song. I like listening to the keyboard. It reminds me of my cousin, Brian, who's a big classic rock fan. The last time that I saw him, he had John Lennon glasses and dressed with the English block-patterned shirts sporting flowered collars.

Then just as my mind is lost in the thoughts of my family, lights surge in the darkness. Is it a mirage? Am I really seeing lights? What are lights doing here in the middle of the desert? Yes, these lights *are* real; they are the lights of a city, the lights of Las Vegas. They suck me in as if I'm an asteroid approaching the sun. The Stratosphere reaches for the sky, hotels line the Strip, and lights sprawl across the valley. There are so many lights! I thought it was just the Strip of hotels, casinos, and strip clubs. People really do live out here.

I follow Javier's directions, which bring me up Las Vegas Boulevard. Mandalay Bay is in the distance, growing in size with each passing mile. I feel like listening to some Frank Sinatra or Dean Martin, but I can't find them on the radio. Why wouldn't they have a radio station playing the Rat Pack all night?

Then it hits me, the proverbial sign. It beacons in the center of the road like a bottle of the bar's finest liquor to an intoxicated fool. "Welcome to Fabulous Las Vegas." A newlywed couple is getting their picture taken in front, with Elvis watching and Big Bird sitting on a stool taking money from kids—a bizarre sight.

Las Vegas is a city that you must visit yourself. Once you see the lights, you forget about all your worries, all your stresses, all your coworkers. Time is different in this city; it slows down, holds you in the moment, and protects you from the outside. You are lost in the desert.

I roll down the window as the heat blasts me. This is the way to do Vegas. This is how they did it in *Vegas Vacation*. I pass the Luxor, the pyramid in the desert. That hotel would only work in one city in the world. A roller coaster loops above the Statue of Liberty. The massive big screen outside the Planet Hollywood ignites the sky. The Eiffel Tower reaches for the stars. Across from it, thousands of people outside the Bellagio watch water spray into the air and dance in the night. Traffic is thick, but creeping along is the perfect speed to take it all in.

People are everywhere. In the crowd, a sexy woman in a miniskirt slinks. Wow! She is so hot. She looks Italian, maybe Greek. She's holding a handbag, her hair flowing in the heat. The lights are making love with her slippery skin. The women on the postcard actually are here in Las Vegas.

A beep blares. I'm drifting into the next lane, so I swerve back, but the light turns red and I have to stop. That was a close one.

Where exactly am I going? Javier says to turn right on Sands Avenue. I look up and see that I'm in front of...Sands Avenue. I hit my right turn signal and turn right on red.

Shit! That sexy woman is in my headlights. I slam on the brakes as she glares at me. Her lipstick is blood red. Wow, she is so hot. She's definitely Italian.

“Get a life, asshole!” she yells, punching my hood, leaving a dent. She sticks her tongue out, showing her tongue ring. Then she opens her mouth and swallows me.

# 6

It's 10:40 on my clock as I pull into the apartment complex. It looks like one of the complexes at Penn State, big parking lot, run-down cars, and overflowing dumpsters. The main difference is the view of the Stratosphere in the background. All the spaces are angled. What is the point of angled parking spaces? You can't pull into an open space if you're going down the aisle in the wrong direction. Just paint the damn lines straight so it's easy to park either way. Are they straight in the mind of the drunk who painted them?

I park and stretch my spine. The heat hits me like when I used to open the oven to steal one of my grandmother's cookies. She used to bake these oatmeal raisin cookies with a touch of cinnamon. I would watch them through the oven window and reach in to grab one with a spatula. Mmm. They were so good. However, as I walk up the steps, my memory of oatmeal raisin cookies in the oven turns into the reality of a half-eaten hamburger on the top step.

I walk across the second level. A burly guy dressed in a sparkling gold shirt and black slacks charges my way so I hug the wall.

"Watch your step," he says.

I keep going. Javier's directions only say the second level, not an exact room number. I'm not going to knock on these doors one by one. I should call Javier, but before I dial, I see a Penn State Nittany Lion on one of the doors.

I knock on the door with three quick taps. The sound of an ambulance echoes in the distance. A high-pitched voice emits from the television in an apartment next door. It sounds like *Family Guy*. I knock again, and then the door opens. There he is, Javier, looking thin with a hint of stubble. He's wearing a robe and smoking a gentleman's pipe. Wow, he hasn't changed in three years. Javier is a mix of a young Hugh Hefner, a carefree Johnny Knoxville, and he shares more than just the first name with Javier Bardem.

"Benjamin, you made it!" he exclaims.

"Javier, you still got the robe and pipe!"

"This is all me. Now, get the hell in here," he says, pulling me inside and giving me a half-hug.

The smell of lemons hits me. The place is big enough to fit a dozen girls and two guys. There's a cheetah-patterned rug surrounded by a brown leather couch, a loveseat, and a huge 32" CRT television—you know, the kind that weighs more than your car. Underneath is a PlayStation 2 with two controllers and a handful of games. There's a coffee table with about twenty empty liquor bottles on display. Most are empty bottles of Jack Daniel's. Further inside, the smell of lemons gets stronger.

"Are you making lemonade?" I ask.

"Just cleaning. I got my old college bud visiting tonight."

The lemons tickle my nose and make me sneeze.

"One more?" Javier goes.

"Huh?"

"You always used to sneeze twice. I remember, man. One small one, and then the monster of all sneezes."

"Ha! You're right. I never thought about it. I guess ever since moving out West, my nose only needs one."

"I guess we all change. Either way, *Gesundheit*, man."

"Thanks," I respond. "It looks like I'm back in our apartment."

"It's one hundred percent bachelor pad. Hey, take a seat and I'll get us a beer," he says, walking into the attached kitchen. Javier always did like the kitchen; it must be a Latino thing.

The leather couch is in front of me, but I don't sit down, because there's too much to look at. In the mix of videos games is *Grand Theft Auto III*. We had a lot of laughs, and made a lot of girls laugh with that game. Against the other wall, there's a desk with a Dell computer. It looks like the older Dimension line from 2003 because it still has the 17" CRT monitor.

"Is that the computer?"

"Oh, yeah. Have at it," Javier goes.

I sit down and turn on the dinosaur. The fans wake up and the monitor makes a big electronic buzz as it flickers on. The Windows XP splash screen greets me. I can hear the hard drive thrashing like it's computing the meaning of life. This old computer is going to take a while to boot.

"I hope you're still not drinking that piss water we always had in college," I say.

"No, I only buy Corona."

"Nice. Good way to start the night."

The Windows XP logo fades to black, showing that I'm close. I glance around the apartment and see a two-foot-tall poster of Grace Kelly. "Is that your room?"

"Nah, my bedroom is in the back. Grace is off limits."

The Windows desktop finally greets me; the wallpaper is a picture of Javier standing in his robe in front of a group of our friends, and there I am with glasses, parted hair, and a sweatshirt. I remember that picture during finals week in 2004, the last time I would see my college friends. It makes me smile.

The icons load and fill the 17" screen. There are icons for Excel and Word documents, pictures, text files, PDF files, three links to solitaire, and a folder labeled, "porn"—I guess he has no one to hide it from. Then like magic, a banner pops up trying to sell me Viagra.

"You always get this message?"

"Oh, yeah, the Viagra ad. Then the thing freezes up after about a minute. I think someone's hacked it."

The first thing you should do when you suspect a virus is to run a full scan with your antivirus software using the latest updates. Javier's computer has no antivirus software. This is a big, big problem. There are free utilities available that work quite good—AVG Antivirus is one.

"I'm downloading this small utility," I say.

The moment I install it and start the auto-protect feature, it pops up with a screen that says, "Virus Detected and Quarantined – E-Mail: How To Tell You're At A Gay Bar."

There's that damn email virus!

"So, you're Latin Lover Two Thousand! You're the ass that sends me all those chain emails. Hey, when did you get this gay-bar email?"

"I got that the other day. Isn't it hilarious?"

"It's a virus! It automatically sends to everyone in your address book."

"Sorry, man. What can I say? Hey, you want a lime?" he asks.

"Yeah, I guess."

Javier springs back into the living room. "Hey, what do you think about Windows Vista? I'm thinking about getting a new computer."

He hands me a cold Corona with a lime. "Thanks, man. Vista is bloated like that chick who used to live next door. You remember the one who would ask you for sugar."

Javier laughs.

"I'd still get XP if you can," I say.

"Good to know. So, did you fix it?"

"Yeah. I'm letting it run a full scan. You gotta watch what you open up."

"Thanks so much! That thing is only good for porn and paying bills."

I move toward the couch and push aside some wrappers, empty cans, and junk mail on the cushion before sitting. There's a stack of *Playboy* magazines on a bookshelf. Is the current issue in there?

Javier raises his beer.

"To your night in Vegas," he says.

"To *our* night in Vegas," I clarify.

We clink glasses. The lime tickles my tastes buds as I suck down a gulp of lost memories. The taste of the alcohol brings me back to a time three years ago, a time where I only worried about my computer science professors and wanting to get laid. Well, I can say the same thing now, but the professors, plural, have turned into the sole professor, Ms. Dipple, and wanting to get laid has turned into *needing* to get laid.

"So how long have you been out here again?" I ask.

"One year this November. I wanted to do something crazy and get away from the snow."

"You go from one extreme to the other."

"Latinos love the heat."

"So what're you doing with your marketing degree?" I ask.

"Promoting. Mainly clubs. Vegas gets more than thirty million visitors a year."

"Business must be good then," I say as I look at the empty liquor bottles on the coffee table.

"It pays the bills."

"So where's your chick?" I ask.

"Hey, you're talking to the Latin lover, remember?"

"So where's your chick?" I repeat.

We share a laugh and a long drink.

"You're lookin' good, man. But you seem...stressed. How are the ladies treating ya in the City of Angels?" Javier says.

"It's more like the City of Devils. I'm single now and probably will be for a long time."

"You just need to get your mojo flowing. Get laid in Vegas and you'll go back to your life a new man."

Javier is right. I need to get laid; that will solve my problems. All this stress, all this aloneness, all this insecurity will be alleviated, placated, removed by a woman's touch. Javier was right there next to me at Penn State, keeping me socially sane as I went academically insane. Computer Science was an excruciatingly hard degree to obtain. The data structures, algorithm design, concrete math, differential equations, programming with C++, logic, and computer networking were enough to push an impressionable great grandson of Czechoslovakian immigrants to the edge, but Javier was there, the gregarious son of Latino immigrants, to pull me back with his wit and women.

I say, "I thought they said, what happens in Vegas…"

"…stays in Vegas. There's a lot about this town that isn't a cliché," Javier finishes.

I take a drink of beer. "Things are so much different out here. Back East, there's not a lot to do and the weather sucks, but you have your friends and family. The West is all about these places with catchphrases and movie connections. In the East, you care about the people; in the West, you care about the places."

"That's some deep shit. Right on, man," he says, taking a drink.

A bang at the door fills the apartment.

"Shit! The cops!" Javier shouts.

I go down. This happened one time during the first week of living with Javier after he fit the description of a man who had bought alcohol for minors (our twenty-year-old neighbors). Javier got out of it because the female cop had a thing for Latinos. However, the pound on this door sounds like it's from a man who is tired, angry, hungry.

I look up and see Javier standing with a smile. That bastard!

"You should've seen your face," he says, laughing.

I sit back down and watch Javier open the door. It's a shadowy figure, wearing a hoodie even though it's ninety degrees outside. Who wears a hoodie in ninety degrees? The man gives Javier a package, and then goes back into the night.

"You still getting visitors with strange packages?" I ask as he places the box on his table.

"I have to work later, just picking up my supplies."

What does a club promoter actually do? It sounds right up Javier's alley. The last time I saw Javier work was at the library as an assistant. His supplies then were his business cards, which he handed to the girls looking for help with the printer. He hooked a few, bringing them back to our place after the library had closed. We shared walls in our apartment; I got good use of noise-cancelling headphones to block out the noises of Javier showing one of these girls his stamp collection. Javier had a big stamp collection, as one girl commented when I bumped into her in the middle of the night on the way to the bathroom. Don't *geeks* have big stamp collections?

"So where are we heading? The Strip?" I ask.

"Nah. The Strip is filled with wannabes. We'll hit up this cool place called, *The Art House*."

"I don't want to meet someone who boils rabbits," I say.

"The women there are all about class. First thing's first. You gotta lose the short sleeves and tie."

“What’s wrong with this?” I ask, checking my polka dot tie.

“That might work on my postmenopausal grandmother, but these women want sophistication.”

“And money.”

“I’ll loan you a shirt. Let’s get started,” he says.

“Hey, whatever happens tonight, I need to call in sick at eight a.m. Or my boss will—”

“Don’t worry. Tonight, forget about your boss,” Javier says.

It’s 11:01 on the clock on the wall. I should be in bed now, but my bed is in another state, on another planet.

Javier raises his beer; we clink glasses and take another swig of Corona. Javier is right; tonight, I’m going to forget about my boss, Ms. *what’s her name*. I keep drinking until the beer is gone.

# 7

The air feels hot on my chest. I'm wearing a long-sleeve blue and black shirt, sleeves rolled up, two buttons undone on my collar, with a splash of cologne called, "OK33." Javier approved of my dress pants and shoes. I added a little gel to my hair, now parted to the right with a twist.

I'm following Javier, my mentor, my fashion designer, my wingman. He's wearing a pink and white shirt with the same look. His hair flows through the night. We walk like Vince Vaughn and Jon Favreau in *Swingers* down the stairs and into the parking lot. I feel good—damn good.

"So, did you buy your Porsche?" I ask.

"Getting there," he goes, gesturing to a mid-nineties Ford Taurus, maroon, rusted around the wheel wells, the front license plate hanging on with one screw.

"You sure got a long way," I say.

"And what are you driving, Bill Gates?"

I point at my Scion, the bus, the brick, the car with low miles and low self-esteem.

"Haha! That's worse than Erectile Dysfunction," he says.

"At least it's new."

"Let's take two cars," he says.

"Come on, it's not that bad."

"Hey, once your dick finds its way, you're on your own."

"Good point. Giddy up," I say.

I get into my car and wait for Javier to lead the way. Following a mid-nineties Ford Taurus reminds me of my high school days. My friend Kevin had a '95 Ford Taurus, dark blue and clean. Back in 1999, the car was only four years old, a Cadillac Escalade to a high school student. I drove an '87 Buick Regal, a hand-me-down. There were many early morning breakfast runs to Burger King before the homeroom bell in that Ford Taurus. They used to have these bite-sized hash browns with their breakfast sandwiches. These little guys would easily slide down when we were running down the hall to beat the bell. Kevin's Ford Taurus looked like the one I'm following now. Time only hurts a car, and it hurts a man if he doesn't let a woman change his oil.

Even though the car is missing a brake light, Javier speeds through the night. We come up to the Stratosphere and get the light red at Las Vegas Boulevard. Javier is first at the light; I am right behind him.

Gobs of people travel across the intersection—an old couple hobbles along, an obese pair with fanny packs ambles, a woman pushes two strollers, three yuppies drink beers and laugh, Asian tourists walk with their heads up high. This is what makes Las Vegas, Las Vegas—the people. Living in Los Angeles, I see diverse people all the time, but Las Vegas brings millions of them together, giving them a Strip of blacktop a few miles long to get lost.

Javier drives for another mile. He turns down Sahara onto a side road called, "Industrial." We're driving in the shadow of the Strip. It's dark here. A man lies on the sidewalk and another guy vomits on the street corner. Where is Javier taking me?

He turns into a secluded parking lot. Low hanging trees cover any markings. As I follow the single brake light, I behold a wide black-and-white three-story building. Lights accent each window, while lush green foliage gives the place life. Mercedes-Benzes and BMWs are parked on each side of us. There's a sign on the canopy, "The Art House."

Javier slows down as two valet attendants stand guard. Men in suits and women in dresses are laughing near the door. I stop behind Javier and get out. Our cars look like someone put two Gap sweaters on a rack of Armani suits.

Before I can say anything to Javier, a pair of Xeon headlights blinds us. It's a red Ferrari. We stand in awe as it pulls around and in front of Javier's car. Its engine calms down like a woman coming down from an orgasm. The color arouses the cones in my eyes. Wow!

The two valet attendants scurry to action. The driver's side opens as a suave man in a gray suit steps out. His hair is slicked back, his face tanned. He stands tall, shoulders back. I can't help but stand tall myself, but the other side of his car stops my heart. A woman's silky legs step out, her skin reflecting even more light than the car. One of the valet attendants helps her up. She's wearing a red dress the same color as her chariot. My eyes land on her cleavage breathing the hot night air, causing the cones in my eyes to ejaculate.

Javier breaks my trance. "And we're not even inside yet."

He leads the way to a valet attendant, a guy who looks a bit off, his black shirt half tucked in. He looks like somebody from a movie. Hmm. I stay back as Javier talks to him, but I can still hear.

"Hey, that's my old college buddy behind me. Here's a ten," he says, but then whispers something I can't understand. What's he saying?!

The man looks at me and whispers something back. Javier reaches into his pocket and gives him another ten.

The man turns toward me and stumbles my way. Yeah, he looks like Forest Gump.

"Hey, my…my…my name is Ch…Chuck and I like brown cars. I want to make it go *vroom…*" He goes for my keys.

I'm not giving Forest Gump my keys!

Javier comes over. "This is Chuck. He really likes brown cars."

That dent on the hood of my car is huge in this light.

Javier snatches the keys and gives them to Forest, who staggers inside my car.

"The party's inside," Javier says.

"Wait. You sure my car will be…" I say, but then Forest revs the car—my car!

Javier pulls me inside.

Replicas of fine art hang on the walls. *Mona Lisa*, *The Starry Night*, *The Scream*, and others I don't recognize offer me their glory. It looks as if there's a hotel front desk at the back wall with two clerks assisting couples. Mysterious sculptures scatter around the floor including a suit of armor guarding a wedding chapel.

As I follow Javier deeper inside, laughter provokes us. Exotic women are conversing and giggling as they make love to loveseats. I'd give my next paycheck to be a loveseat right now.

"Wow, they never showed this place in the Vegas ads. Am I in SoHo?" I say.

"I knew you'd like it," he replies.

"What is this place exactly?"

"Hotel, restaurant, lounge."

More females chuckle. I follow my ears and see two ladies in black dresses melting in leather chairs with wine in their hands and in their blood.

"Those chicks will cost you," Javier mutters.

"Do you think they'll take a check?"

"Come on, let's hit the lounge."

Before I turn to follow my Latin leader, a figure on the wall catches me. Its colors and its swirls scream.

"*The Scream* by Edvard Munch. My favorite," I say.

"Save the art talk for the ladies." Javier leads me toward the sound of smooth jazz hidden behind two curtains.

Abruptly, a man with long hair in a ponytail parts the curtains and stares me down. He's tall, easily 6'5", and he wears a stone face. He's the villain in a Bond movie. As his eyes shift to Javier, he cracks a smile.

"Javier. How are you?" he says with a thick Eastern European accent.

"Fabulous. Hey, I want you to meet my old college roommate at Penn State. This is Benjamin," Javier introduces.

I shake his hand. It's cold like raw fish from the market, but at least he's smiling.

"This is Vincent. From..." Javier goes.

"Czech Republic," the manager says.

See, he is the perfect Bond villain. Weren't there a few villains from the Czech Republic?

"A pleasure," I say. "My great grandparents were from Czechoslovakia. I was brought up on Haluski, Halupki."

"Pierogies," he adds.

"Mmm, my favorite."

"I don't know how you guys can eat all that starch on starch," Javier says.

This guy is a perfect example of an Eastern European, a specimen born and bred during the communist days. These people were taught to wear poker faces, to hold their cards back and only reveal them to an ally. They are cold, abrupt, and raw when you meet them, but once the introduction has been made, they reveal their hands. I like this guy, even though thirty seconds ago he bothered me. He reminds me of my family back in Pennsylvania. The grandchildren of Eastern Europe still flourish in the Pocono Mountains. I grew up Byzantine Catholic and went to school with kids whose last name rhymed with *thick* or *stock*. Now, I'm in the most diverse place in America, even the world. There are people all around me, but this man named Vincent from the Czech Republic makes me realize how alone I am.

"So how could anyone live with this rabid animal?" the manager says, inducing laughter.

"Earplugs and Lysol spray," I reply, evoking even more laughter.

"Well, enjoy, gentlemen. The crowd is diverse tonight," the manager says as he holds open the curtain to the crypt.

Javier leads the way. A DJ is spinning records in the corner. His sound makes me feel like I'm watching the *Local on the 8s* on The Weather Channel with every day showing hot and humid. Candles flicker off the artwork, sculptures, and crowd. Some sit on couches with drinks, and some have drinks and cigars, while others chatter around the bar. The crowd is young, twenties and thirties. I feel alive. It's as if I'm dreaming, yet this is better than any dream I've had.

"Let's check out the bar," Javier says.

There are mirrors and paintings attached to the ceiling. How did they secure them? We slide past a group of young women, a sweet scent of sex slipping inside me. The girl with the porcelain skin looks hot. She has perfect cleavage, and she catches me looking, but I don't care.

We sit down at the rectangular bar with a view of the crowd, an empty seat next to each of us. The wood is old, the type found in the art district bars in New York City. I caress the bar and feel the energy of the porcelain girl flowing through the wood and into my fingers. Does she feel me?

A magnetic female bartender dressed in a corset and leather pants gravitates toward us. "Gentlemen, what are we having?" she asks.

"Wine," Javier says.

Wine sounds good.

"Do you need a wine list?" she asks.

"No, two glasses of the house Merlot, please."

"A bottle is actually the same price as two glasses."

"That's the bargain of the night," I say.

"You'd better bring four glasses with that bottle," Javier says.

"You got it," she replies, and then fetches our drinks.

I grab my wallet. I hope I have enough money. I hit the ATM yesterday at lunch after that Subway sandwich, but I was not anticipating a trip to Vegas. I'd gotten one hundred out. How far will a hundred get me tonight? If it's anything like in college with Javier, not far.

"Let me get it," Javier says.

"*You* actually offering to pay?"

"I'm a working man now."

Javier offering to pay is like a homeless man giving *you* his change at a red traffic light.

"Nah, this one's on me." It's a nice gesture, a long overdue gesture, but as they say, it's the *gesture* that counts. As I grab a twenty, Javier snatches my work I.D. from my wallet.

"Ha! Oh my God, you've got to be kidding!" he says, studying it.

Suddenly, Ms. Dipple's obnoxious laugh surrounds me. Her hot breath hits my shoulder and her fermented stench punches me. Anything can happen to *me*, but my badge…no! I should have left it back in LA, but I never had the chance to stop at home.

"Hey, be careful! If I lose that, I—"

"Don't go postal on me, man. This looks like a mug shot."

The coating on the badge reflects the low light as gold would. "I feel like I'm in an episode of *The Twilight Zone* at my job. One day, I'm going to wake up and find myself aged twenty years."

"I think I saw that one."

"Life gets much more complicated after college. It's tough to find your identity, especially when some people still buy you Happy Meals."

"Who the hell buys you Happy Meals?" he asks.

The barn door has just opened. A lot has changed over the past three years. When you're in your twenties, you see life through an amplifier, searching for some meaning to your daily routine. You study every coworker, family member, acquaintance over the age of forty and picture yourself in their shoes. Which path are you going to take? Will you end up being the fifty-year-old uncle who never marries? Will you become the forty-year-old colleague who talks about his four kids and his mortgage payments next to you at the urinal? Or will you end up being the fifty-five-year-old next door neighbor who wishes he had life to do over again until the day he dies prematurely of a heart attack? Being in your twenties is the most terrifying time in your life.

The bartender arrives, bringing me back to the moment. I'm not going to think about my problems anymore!

She sets down the four glasses and opens the bottle.

"Just fill two for now," Javier says as she pours.

"Those for your alter ego?" I ask.

"For our hot bitches. I'll show you how it's done."

The bartender finishes pouring my glass, and then smiles coyly. "Good luck, gentlemen."

The glass feels cool. Inside, the deep red liquid absorbs the light. If the liquid had a name, it would be Alessandra.

"Forget about all your shit. Tonight is your night," Javier goes.

"To a night that never ends," I say, raising my glass.

"Now I'll drink to that."

We clink glasses, the sound louder than the bass bellowing in the room. Then I kiss Alessandra and let her enter my body. The music seems to get louder, or maybe it's because I'm getting softer. The paintings on the wall absorb me. My favorite is the one showing a large fish with human legs. Is it a mermaid? What's the opposite of a mermaid?

The laughs from the swirling crowd change my focus. There's an Asian guy; he looks Korean. He's enticing two ladies to laugh. What's he saying to them? I wish I had the discrete surveillance kit with me that I had bought last year online. You could wear an earbud and conceal the receiver in your sleeve. By simply pointing it in the direction of interest, you could hear a specific conversation from 30 feet away, even through a crowded room. Ahh, what am I thinking about? I should just go over there if I want to know what they're discussing!

"Awesome place. I'm surprised they don't have a dance floor," I say.

"*You*, dance?" he goes.

"If the song's right, I'll bust a groove." Other than a choreographed routine in high school, I've only danced a couple of times in public—one being at my cousin's wedding in PA. After my grandmother fell off her chair, I stopped.

"I'd pay to see that." Javier takes a drink of wine, a long drink. "So, are you going to make your move? There're a lot of eligible bitches here."

"That group when we walked into the bar looked pretty enticing." The cleavage on that girl with the porcelain skin consumes my brain. She's around here somewhere. I check next to me, but see only the empty chair. Where is she hiding?

"I'm your wingman tonight," he says.

"I bet you don't even know what a *wingman* is," I reply.

"It's textbook, Benny. Let's say I'm your wingman, which means you're getting the hot one tonight. This works when you find the ugly girl. Remember, the ugly girl always has a hot friend. The problem is that this hot friend is untouchable. If you approach her, she's never going to go with you because she would never leave her ugly friend."

"Keep going," I say, sipping my wine.

"That's where your wingman comes in. I go for the ugly one first. That way, her hot friend can open up and relax. Then you come along and I introduce you to the two girls. The next step is very important."

"This is fascinating." I take another drink of wine.

"The wingman must immediately invite the ugly one to a private area. She will be flattered and will always go. Of course, her hot friend will go too. Then… Bam! You're automatically invited. So now, *you* get a lot of alone time with the hot one. This is your time to shine, the time that every guy in the bar wishes he had."

"That is actually pretty ingenious. I'm impressed," I say.

"Remember, man. None of your pussy shit. For tonight, you're a different person. You're Javier."

He's right. I'm in his town, in his bar, in his clothes. I can be whoever I want to be. Why not be a Latin Lover with more girls notched on his belt than computers he has fixed?

"*Me llamo Javier*. I would like to make passionate love to you," I say with my best Latin accent.

"Ha! Come on, I'm not that bad."

I rub my fingers across my chin and say, "I forgot to add the chin squeeze on my stubble." Wait, I don't have any stubble.

The song changes to one with more bass. It's enough to raise my head, and as I do, a sight in front of me makes me feel Alessandra sliding through my veins. Two tall and tempting females slink through the crowd. One is Asian, an island girl with sun-kissed skin exposed to the air, a black dress hiding her naughty parts. The other girl is a runway model, an African-American, the candles getting lost in her black skin. And they're both coming our way.

"Hey, there we go," Javier says.

"Wow," I utter. "What happens to your wingman theory when there's no ugly one?"

"It's every man for himself. You can have the black girl," Javier says.

If I had to choose blindly, I'd choose both, but the Asian girl piques my interest. Asians like computers. Perhaps she is a computer geek too. Tall, tempting, and techy—I'm going to wet my pants.

"I'm kinda digging the Asian," I say.

"Look at the way the black girl moves. How about that bouncing on your rod?" Javier says.

The girls stop two chairs away from me at the bar and wait for the bartender. Sweat forms on my brow. I hate this moment—the moment of truth. It's all about the guy now. He has to cast his line at the exact spot to hook the fish. The problem for me is that I don't know how to fish. I barely know how to swim, seriously! But I have Javier here, my wingman. He has the biggest pole. Wait a second… Did I just think that!

He grabs the two empty glasses and winks at me. I wipe my brow. He slides over to the ladies. This guy is a genius.

"Why wait, ladies? I knew you were coming so I already got you a glass," he goes.

"Nice try, Rico Suave. I've heard better pick-up lines," the black girl says.

The master gets shut down! I think his approach is too pointed. Not that I should know, a man who hasn't been laid west of the Mississippi, but tonight I am not that man; I am suave, cool. I think I know what to say, but my palms are sweaty. I can't shake a woman's hand with sweaty palms. I look up at that Korean guy making the girls laugh. They're still laughing. I can do this. What the hell, right? The problem that I see is that Javier forgot the most important thing. The two ladies need a new girlfriend named Alessandra. Grabbing the bottle, I walk between them and pour two glasses.

"The truth is that we bought a bottle of wine in anticipation of meeting some lovely ladies at the bar. The bottle's still full and you both look lovely."

"A realist. I like the way this one operates," the black girl says.

I'm sandwiched between these girls. Their slippery scents swirl around me and send me into an aura. This is really working. The Asian girl's skin looks so soft. Her hair brushes against my shirt. A woman this hot must have come from a faraway land.

"*Ha ji me ma shi te*?" I say.

She shakes her head.

"*Ni hao ma*?" I say.

"Try, *how do you do*?" she says as she moves closer to Javier.

Did I offend her? This whole suave thing is harder than it looks. As my gut twists, I realize that there is another half to this situation. She's dark like chocolate and she's looking at me. My grandmother was right; there are other fish in the sea.

The bartender swings by and sees us. She gives me a wink.

I exhale and say to the black girl, "I'm Benjamin."

"Benjamin, huh? You look like a Bill," she replies.

"How can someone look like a name?"

"They just can."

"Well, what came first? The name or the look?"

"Bill Gates. That's it. You look like a younger version of him," she goes.

She's on to me. She knows that I'm not this cool guy who hangs out in the clubs. I have to be cool, so I take a sip of wine and say, "I do get that a lot. I should check my bank account."

"I'm Jazmin," she says.

I got a name! I got a name! "I've never met a Jazmin before."

"Well, now you have." She offers me her hand. She has those French-manicured nails. You know, the ones with the perfectly squared white tips. Her fingers look like fingers of steel. How are you supposed to grip a lady's hand when you first meet her? Is the whole underhanded grip still in fashion? I know the kiss is too much, unless you're just having fun. A normal handshake just seems so professional. What about strength? Should I grip it softly? I don't want her to think I'm weak. Should I squeeze it tightly? I don't want to scare her off, make her think there's a maniac inside of me. I should've asked Javier this, but it's too late now. What would Javier do?

I accept her hand, gripping it at the knuckles, and give it a slight squeeze.

"So, what do you do, Benjamin?" she asks.

It must've worked, but now the proverbial question. Should I lie? Am I Javier or Benjamin? Taking too long will make her think I'm lying. I say, "Information Systems Policy Analyst."

"Is that computers?" she asks.

"Yeah, mainly."

"I know someone who does that. You don't seem like you're from here."

She can see through me! I'm just going to be myself. I can't hold it any longer.

"Well, you're right. I just drove in from LA."

"Wow, Hollywoodland. So, what brought you here?"

My grandmother was right when she said just be yourself. I should've listened to her more. "I needed one night to get away. To explore."

"Explore, huh? Explore what?" she says. I glance into her velvet eyes. Wow, they are so sexy. I can see myself in them.

"Your eyes are beautiful," I say.

She looks away and exhales a quick little burst through her nose. Is she nervous? "This wine tastes so good," she says.

"Yeah, there's a hint of some berry in it."

"You're right. A berry," she says.

"Huckleberry, maybe?"

"Huckleberry?" she replies.

"Yeah, I think."

"Out of all the berries, you choose a *huckleberry*? What the hell is a huckleberry anyway?"

"Everyone knows what a huckleberry is. Your grandmother never baked you huckleberry pie?"

She nods her head repeatedly and says, "Yeah, she baked me a pie and put it by the open window to cool, but a big bad wolf stole it."

"I think you're confusing your children's stories. I'm certain you've had huckleberries before."

"How do you know that? Really, how do you know that?" she says, setting down the wine glass and lacing her fingers.

"I'm one hundred percent certain you've had one, and you've enjoyed it."

"Enough with the huckleberries!" she snaps back.

My right foot jackhammers the floor. Stop babbling, Benjamin! This is going all wrong!

Suddenly, her Asian friend laughs out loud. Javier is stroking the soft skin on her back. "Oh, the artist is at work," I say.

"My friend is really easy," Jazmin says.

I bite my lip. I told Javier that I wanted the Asian one! I knew it. He's not getting my back; he's here just for himself. I even paid for the wine. See, this is all part of his plan. Nothing has changed with this guy in three years. Why do I always listen to him? I should never have come here. I take a long gulp of wine.

"But don't worry. I'm just as horny," Jazmin's voice slides into my ear and constricts me. I choke on the wine and start coughing hard. She pounds on my back. "It's okay, baby."

I clear my throat and take a deep breath. This is going to happen. This woman wants me. That's right, she's horny, and she wants Benjamin Pollock, a twenty-six-year-old geek. My penis gets hard as her words finally snake their way to my crotch.

"So, how do you want to do this?" I whisper to her.

Before she can send more sound waves my way, a beep from her purse steals her focus. "Hold that thought," she says as she checks her cell phone. It's one of those new iPhones. Why do these sexy women love iPhones? It's a tech guy's gadget, the Internet, text, chat, calculations, apps all in one easy-to-carry device. Oh, and it makes calls too.

The light from the phone bathes her face. Damn, her lips look so moist. They're painted in a color of red that I've only seen when looking at the sun. How would it be to kiss those lips, to feel their juiciness against my skin? But then, she takes those lips and contorts them into an expression that I detest, an expression that I've seen before when I was this close to a woman, the last expression I want to see—a failing frown.

"Something suddenly came up," she says.

"Isn't that Marcia's line from *The Brady Bunch*?" I say, scratching the back of my head.

"What?"

"Never mind, I knew a woman of your caliber was out of my league."

She leans over again as I hold my breath.

"Sweetie, I love computer geeks," she whispers, but something has changed in her voice. No longer does it grip my body; my body rejects it. For some reason, I am mad at myself. I should have brought that other new device with me, the one that blocks cell phone signals within a six-foot proximity. If I had it activated in my pocket, I could have blocked the signal of binary ones and zeros from infiltrating her phone. I didn't know at the time why I bought it, but now I know, and it's too late. I should have left that thing in my car. Why am I so stupid?!

"Give me your number and I'll text you later," she says.

"I know you're just being nice. I understand."

"If you're really someone else, forget it," she says.

The music gets thicker. The smell of something chalky strangles me. Why am I here? Who am I? I'm Benjamin Pollock.

"You think I'd lie about being a computer geek?" I say.

I show her my Pegman Telecom I.D. from my wallet. This is who I am, an Information Systems Policy Analyst, visiting a city that probably doesn't know what that title is.

"Okay, I believe you," she says. "Let me put your number into my phone. Call me so I have it."

She hands me a business card. It's white and even though the light is dim inside this place, I can see written in black: "Jazmin – 702.468.2223." That's all it says. I've seen hundreds of business cards in the past three years working at Pegman Telecommunications, but I've never seen one like this.

I do as she instructs me, and then her fingers with French-manicured nails snatch the card away. "My last one. I'll text you later, sweetie."

Then like that, she leaves me with nothing. Jazmin stands and interjects herself between her friend and Javier. She must really have to go.

Javier turns to me. Gone is the scent of the sexy Jazmin, replaced by the musky Javier. "You scared her away already?"

"She said something suddenly came up."

"Benny, Benny, Benny, I need to have a talk with you," Javier says, shaking his head.

We watch Jazmin leave. What does he want me to do? I'm trying here. Before I can say anything, the Asian girl caresses his back. Now all I can do is watch.

Javier turns and kisses her passionately. It's one of those movie kisses, her hands cupping his face as her tongue explores. I can't watch this. This is disgusting.

"I'll meet you out front, baby. I need to use the little girls' room," she says to him, loud enough for me to hear. She wants to rub this in. She whispers something else into his ear, and then like that, she slides away. Her hips sway to the music, which seems to have gotten faster as I've slowed down.

"She's inviting me over to her place," Javier says.

"I told you I wanted the Asian one," I say.

"Benjamin, it's all in the way you approach them."

"Well, *you* didn't start out very well."

"It's about what and how you say it. Women dig funny with a hint of cockiness. It's in your delivery."

"Funny with a hint of cockiness. Hmm…" I take a deep breath.

"Remember, man, you're in Vegas. You're no longer Benjamin Pollock, the introverted computer geek. You're Benjamin Pollock, the confident visiting businessman."

"But where's my red Ferrari?"

"Just pretend you're in a movie."

Javier gives me a key from his pocket. I hope it's not the key to his heart. "Well, I'm out. If you need to use my place, here's an extra key. Good luck." Javier scurries out, his tempo outpacing the music.

Now I'm alone. I always end up alone. Javier is right. I should be a new and improved Benjamin Pollock worth his weight in gold. I'm in a movie. This whole scene is from a movie I've seen, or will see. I need to say things that are funny with a hint of cockiness. I can do that, like James Bond or Ethan Hunt, but those guys are already cast. I just need to figure out my persona. Decide on this now, so I can play him out when the ladies arrive. I just need to focus, to become this character, and then this new Benjamin will be smooth in conversation, know what to say, and when to say it. But who will I become?

The bartender comes back. She sees me all by myself. "You finished?"

Even though I'm alone, it's not even midnight. This day is not even over. There are still hours before the sun will rise. "Nah, I'll be back. Oh, I have a question. Are there huckleberries in your house Merlot?"

She furrows her brow and says, "Are you fuckin' serious?"

# 8

Is this sword real? I'm afraid to find out. The suit of armor looks as if a Knight of the Round Table wore it. The metal on the chest reflects the spotlights. I touch it with my fingertips, finding that it's cold. This sword has to be real. I go closer to it. The tip looks like the tip of a dagger. I extend my finger, closer and closer, but then I hear someone clear his throat. I retreat, but there is no one else around me in this lobby other than a couple on the couch and two clerks behind the front desk. Did I just hear that? Is there someone inside this suit of armor?!

I go over to the clerks. "Excuse me, where's your restroom?" I ask the female one with a crooked nose.

She points toward the back.

As I make my way to rejuvenate myself, I see through the front doors. There's Javier and the Asian girl laughing with that valet attendant, Forest Gump. Hey, he's talking normal! He's not retarded! I can hear their laughs through the glass. Those bastards! I hate Javier. I always did. I just pretended not to. I should've listened to the boring little Benjamin on my shoulder; he was boring, but he had dignity.

I go to the men's room. The door is made of wood so thick and dark that it looks as if I'm entering some chamber in a medieval mansion. The door even creaks.

Inside, a large mirror adds depth to the confined space. A small vending machine with mints and aspirins hangs on the wall. I shift to a urinal and unzip.

The sound of silence surrounds me. Nothing happens. Come on. No one's in here. Just piss! I whistle. A trickle starts, but then the door squeaks open and I stop the stream.

Footsteps enter. They sound strange, like a pendulum. I turn my head as the silky woman from the red Ferrari clinks in. What?! Am I in the women's room? Why is there a urinal in the women's room?

"Oops," she says, and then darts out.

I wish she didn't go. I'm ready to pee again, but the door opens. This time, the steps are more prominent. It's the suave man from the red Ferrari, the silky woman's date.

"Sorry, bud. My lady had a little too much, too fast."

He stands next to me, and then pees like a shaken champagne bottle that was just uncorked. I start to pee too.

"That was the second time someone walked in on me today," I say.

"It must be a sign."

"A sign to call it a night," I say as I flush.

The sink is a giant soup bowl. The only other time I've seen one of these was in the men's room at The Beverly Hilton. I wash and finish with a splash of water on my face. My eyes are so red. I need sleep, but my bed is five hours away.

The man joins me.

"How did you snag that hot woman?" I ask.

"Women like flash," he says as he fixes his collar and adjusts the rolls in his sleeves.

"You mean the red Ferrari?" I look down at my blue and black shirt and realize it's not even mine.

"Flash can come in many forms."

The suave man slides his masculine hands through his hair and combs his eyebrows with his fingers. "Let me ask you a question," he goes, looking at me through the mirror. "When you're trying to make a left at a green light, and you're waiting there for your turn, do you wait behind the line? Or do you scoot up so you can still sneak through when the light turns yellow?"

I just stare at him through the mirror. What does he mean?

"Good luck, bud," he says as he leaves.

His question is so bizarre. Hmm. I never scoot up at the green light, because I'm too afraid.

My image in the mirror reflects back at me, but I keep seeing Benjamin Pollock. For the rest of this night, I'm not the old Benjamin Pollock. I'm the suave man with the red Ferrari who doesn't stay behind the line. I slick my hair back with some water, roll up my sleeves, and comb my eyebrows with my fingertips. I take a deep breath. The lingering cologne of the suave man energizes my soul. Round two…

I go back to the bar. The lights seem dimmer, the perfect place to play. I stand tall as the music surrounds me. This song is great. I give a thumbs-up to the DJ. The crowd is buzzing. The porcelain girl is still talking to her friends. I wink at her. It feels great to wink. I caress the wood on the bar, absorbing all the energy, all the sex appeal.

As my eyes take it all in as if through a fisheye lens, there's something different in front of me. As I get closer to my seat, the seat where I left Benjamin Pollock the geek, and am returning Benjamin Pollock the suave man, I see someone sitting there. It's a woman, but it's not just any woman. She's tall, even though she is sitting. Her layered hair is sharp, needlelike. Her lips are moist, fattened, and she has blue eyes that are staring at me.

I take a seat next to her and pour myself another glass of wine. I sneak a sniff of the woman's scent, as my brain overclocks. Something is hidden inside her aroma, something dark, something that begs to be uncovered.

She's drinking a vodka martini; I've seen it before in a drink book. I grab my wine and prepare to say something cool. The right words are ready to come out, but before I can speak, she speaks first.

"I was waiting for your *friend* to leave," she says with an Eastern European accent.

I hold the wine in my mouth. Did she just say that?

"What's that?" I ask.

"I said I was waiting for your *friend* to leave so I could come over. I was watching you."

I swallow hard. This is too good to be true. She must have the wrong guy. Where is she from? Poland? Czech Republic? No, sounds more mysterious.

"You sure you've got the right guy? I didn't see you before."

"But I saw you."

"You have quite the sexy accent. Is that Russian?" I ask.

She leans toward me. The darkness in her scent jolts my brain. Who is this woman?

"The party starts at midnight," she whispers.

What's she talking about? I glance at my watch. "I only got eleven forty five."

My face reflects in her eyes. Oh, those eyes are deadly.

"Are you the man for me?" she asks.

What the hell is she talking about? I look across the bar and see the suave man. He holds his drink up and nods at me as he strokes his silky woman. I peek at this Russian woman's legs. They're so smooth. Then it hits me. This is a game, and I like games, so I nod back at the suave man.

"Yes, I am that man, sweetie. What is your name?" I say.

"Natasha."

I take her hand; it's as cold as ice. I bring it up and rest my lips on her skin. She tastes better than wine. "It's a pleasure, Natasha. You are quite the temptress."

"We must do this discreetly," she says.

I like how this girl thinks. She wants to play the Bond girl, and I am Mr. Bond. "Discretion is my middle name."

She takes another sip of her drink, so I follow her lead.

"I like you. You're not like the others," she says with that killer accent.

"Darling, I'm all about the finer things in life. I'd like to add you to my collection," I say with a smirk formed by muscles that I've never used before.

"We should go up to my room."

"Oh, you're staying here?"

"Yes, I have the da Vinci Suite."

"Very nice. Did you see my red Ferrari outside?" I say.

"You have a red Ferrari?"

"Of course. Remember I'm all about flash—I mean class."

"I thought guys with small penises get a red Ferrari."

"No… They get a yellow one. Red is reserved for the larger men."

"Is that right?" Her pupils dilate.

"I'm a man of mystery, my dear."

"Well, can I have your package?"

Wow, this woman is blunter than a kick in the crotch. She could be one of those women who needs a one-night stand, one of those women whose boyfriend just cheated on her, one of those women who only cares about a dick and not whether it's attached to a geek. I could be that dick. Maybe the dice has rolled in my favor on this one, and I'm either going to go home rich or be taken home poor. Either way, this is fun.

"A direct woman. I like that," I say.

"Let's do this upstairs in my room," she says.

"My next words exactly."

The bartender stops by. She looks at me with a blank expression. What's going through her mind? She nods at Natasha. "You're doing okay?"

"Ask her that in about ten minutes," I answer for her, winking at the bartender.

Okay, I shouldn't press my luck.

The bartender smiles, showing her dimples. "Have fun."

I leave a twenty for the bartender. I stand up first and help Natasha. She's tall, must be 5'9" without heels, but she's wearing heels. She's also wearing a black dress with vertical lines cut out over her hips to give a peek at what lies beneath. Her breasts look about a C-cup, but then again, I've only seen a C-cup in the movies; I've only touched a small B at best, and that was with only one eye open.

Natasha holds my hand; it's so hot. Did I warm her up that much? Or maybe *I've* cooled down. We step as one around the couples, through the drunken laughs, between the cigar smoke. I walk next to her as if I'm the prize and she is one of Barker's Beauties. The suave man gives me a thumbs-up. The DJ smiles and nods, doing a little record scratch for me. This is living. However, as I escape through the curtains, the music fades, and the laughs die out. It's different out here, but at this point, I'm just going to roll with it.

As soon as my finger hits the up arrow, the elevator opens. I let her go on to make the decision. She presses "3" as I stand back and just live in the moment.

Suddenly, the manager scurries our way and yells, "Hold the elevator, please!"

I prop it open, letting him on. He hits the number "2" as the elevator closes. Then, there are three.

As we ascend, Natasha hides behind me. What is she doing? The manager glances over, but Natasha clutches my back. Is she hiding from him? Maybe he's her boyfriend. See, I knew there was something going on with this woman. It was all too good to be true. However, as my mind clouds with variables, Natasha spins me and engulfs me with her lips. She kisses deeply, her warmth transferring through me. Seconds pass, which seem like hours. By the time I turn around, the manager has already gotten off and we are at her floor.

"Wow," I expel.

"He doesn't know *you*, but he knows *me*," she says.

"Who? The manager from the Czech Republic?"

She pulls my hand. "Quickly. We need to get to my room."

"I like your style," I say, too aroused to think.

I follow her down the red-carpeted hallway. Artwork lines our path. It smells like old wood from the White Birch trees lining my backyard growing up. I like this woman—not only because she likes me, but also because she is quirky, a geek in a dress. My heart is racing. My eyes are wide, yet a part of me is terrified to look.

We make it to an ominous door with the words *da Vinci Suite*. As she unlocks it, I see my reflection in a mirror down the hallway. The color red paints my face, remnants of her lipstick. The image makes me smile.

She opens the door. The Benjamin who walks through this door will walk out a different man.

As we enter, Natasha begins checking behind the bed and nightstand. It's darker than a catacomb in here. How can she see in the dark? I grab a matchbook from the table and light a candle in the middle of the room. I put the matchbook in my back pocket, a keepsake to remember the moment—as if I will ever forget this moment! The candle burns, bouncing light off *The Last Supper*, the *Mona Lisa*, and *Virgin of the Rocks*. So this is why they call it the da Vinci Suite.

"This is a sweet suite. What is it you do exactly?"

She turns to me, a different Natasha from the bar. She has a priority in her eyes. She must really want it. I take a seat on the bed. It's firm, perfect for lovemaking.

"Place looks clean. Do you have it?" she says.

What is she talking about? Wait. I know what it is. I keep one in my wallet for a rainy day, or a hot night in Vegas. At least I think I have one.

"Let me check," I say.

I open my wallet to a couple of twenties, insurance cards for my car and my health, my CVS ExtraCare card, and my work I.D. Where is it?! I always keep one in here. I sure as hell didn't use it. "Shit. I don't have one, do you?"

"What are you talking about?" she says.

"Condoms."

"Condoms?" she whips back.

This is going the wrong way. I need to back this up, to bring us back to the bashful banter at the bar. The flame is bouncing off her silky legs. I reach over to pet them, but she jumps back and pulls a pistol on me. What the fuck?! Oh my God. I have a pistol pointed at me!

"Whoa! Okay. I'll go get some," I say.

"Forget the damn condoms! Who are you?"

"I'm Benjamin Pollock from Los Angeles."

"You're not the *Handler*?"

"Yeah, I thought..." I begin saying. Isn't this part of her game? I thought we were playing Bond and Bond girl. Is that gun real?! "...the Handler? No, I'm an Information Systems Policy Analyst."

"I don't believe you. Who sent you?"

"Sent me? I came with Javier."

"Javier from the cartel?" she says, furrowing her brow.

"No, Javier from Penn State," I clarify.

She tightens her grip on the gun. Its barrel pierces my soul. I could be dead any second now. All she needs to do is flex her pointer finger, and then I'm finished. I don't want to die! I'm just a computer geek playing a game. I reach into my pocket to grab my wallet, but she waves the gun at me.

"Whoa! Whoa!" I say with my wallet in hand. "No, see, look. This is my work badge. I just thought the innuendo was part of your sexual foreplay."

She snatches my work I.D. "Nice picture."

"So, I don't want to know anything. I don't know you. I never saw you before. This all never happened."

She throws the I.D. at me. I put it back into its holster.

A gun pointed at you feels like you're trapped underwater with your breath running out. It's weird; once it's planted on you, you lose focus on the person behind it. It's just you and the gun.

"Why don't you go look for a girl at the corner of walk and don't walk," she says, putting the gun down on the nightstand.

"Huh?" I reply.

"Get the hell out of here!" she yells.

I go to turn, but I can't help but admire her black dress. It really does accentuate her hourglass figure. I lick my lips and taste the lip-gloss on my mouth, her lip-gloss! "By the way, you're such a great kisser. I never—"

"Get out!" she snaps.

"Okay. Okay."

Then I leave…alone. I can't believe that room, that woman. No one's going to believe what just happened to me, but no one has to know; no one should know. I can't believe that she questioned my identity. Couldn't she see through my act? I guess not. Bizarrely, this energizes me.

As I wait for the elevator, I don't think about me; I think about her. Although she questioned my identity, my intentions, the real question is—who the hell is she?

# 9

What kind of leather is this? It's so soft. My body conforms to it. What are the different types of leather? Does leather from an abused cow, fed scraps from the bottom of the barrel, feel differently than leather from a cow that grazed the organic pastures? Does leather from a female cow feel differently than from a male cow? This leather is so soft, so supple. It's like warm butter between my legs. This must be a female cow, a sexy cow.

What the hell am I thinking about? My eyes are so heavy. A yawn escapes my mouth. It's 12:13 on my watch. The new day has begun. I should just go back to Javier's place and crash on his couch. I'll set my alarm for 8:00, no, 8:03, and then call in sick. Ms. Dipple will have to excuse me. There's no other choice, because I'm a half-day drive away from work, a half-day drive away from my life.

I stand up from this chair in the lobby of The Art House. It's quiet in here. It's just me, the paid front desk workers, and a hundred eyes of subjects painted by dead artists. Oh yeah, and there's that knight in shining armor. I don't want to go near that thing. The music behind the curtains has no effect on me. I'm done with this place.

As I walk toward the door, I smell smoke. Is something on fire? It's not cigar or cigarette smoke. Something's definitely burning. I investigate down a hallway lined with a massive bookcase. Wow, there are tons of books here, including the drawings of Leonardo da Vinci, a dozen Lewis Carroll books, and a collection of Edgar Allan Poe.

The smoke is coming from behind a door, cracked open an inch. The lights are on inside, and the smoke billows out. It doesn't smell like a wood fire or plastic. It's smoke with flavor.

I inch closer to the door and see shadows shifting inside. Something is going on in there. I'm four feet away as I hear a crack and the moan from a man inside. Through the slit in the door, I see a naked man lying on a table. A petite woman wearing a sports bra and shorts is standing on his back, walking as if she's walking the plank. Incense is burning, causing the smoke. The woman twists her right foot; his bones crack and he groans. Oh my God! I don't know whether he's loving it or loathing it. I'm getting out of here!

As I flee the hallway, a book from the bookcase falls to the floor and opens. It's the Bible open to John, Chapter 9. My eyes lock onto a passage. I whisper it aloud, "Whereas once I was blind, now I can see."

A beep blasts from my pocket. This is all too weird, man. I put the book back and check my phone. "One New Text Message." It says, "Let's go to a Swingers Club – Jazmin."

"Unbelievable," I utter.

What exactly is a swingers club? Does everyone swing on a swing? I'm sure it's something adult. One of those iPhones would be helpful right about now. I could Google it. I need to buy one when my contract is up. Damn, what does this text mean? I go back to the bookcase and check for an encyclopedia, but the moment more moans pour from that room, I retreat.

There's a short Hispanic man pushing a cart. He stops to empty a trashcan.

"Excuse me," I say.

He points toward the bathroom.

"No, I have a question for you."

He puts down the trashcan.

"Do you know what a swingers club is?"

"*Qué*?" he says.

"*Donde está swingers club*?" I ask using my high school Spanish skills.

"Swingers club?" he repeats with a thick accent.

"*Sí*."

"Hmm," he exhales. Another custodial worker is pushing a cart of laundry bags.

"*Raul, donde está swingers club*?" the worker asks.

"Ahh," he exhales, and then spouts off words in Spanish a mile a minute.

"What's he saying?" I ask.

The second worker grabs a laundry bag and starts humping it. "Swingers club. Pretty girls."

Both men laugh. I shake my head. "*Gracias, amigos.*" They continue their mundane jobs.

I'm sold. If that laundry bag were Jazmin's body bent over a chair, I would be in heaven. So she *was* sincere deep down. I could tell by the way that she had whispered to me, her slippery sound seizing my soul.

I reply to her text with "Where?"

If I go to the club, I'm going to need protection, and lots of it. Perhaps Jazmin is just the tip of the iceberg. I walk to the front desk worker, the one with the crooked nose.

"Still looking for that restroom?" she says.

"Uh, no. I found it. But I am actually looking for something else," I say with tact.

"What?" she replies, eyes squinted.

"Do you know where I can buy a..."

"A..."

I lean in so the other front desk worker doesn't hear. He looks like a meathead with a chip on his shoulder. His shaved skull gives him away. I whisper to her, "Condom."

"Oh, well, we actually sell them in the restrooms."

"Really? I didn't see them."

"They should be there in a vending machine on the wall."

"Thanks," I say, adding a wink. Crooked nose or not, she's okay in my book. Maybe I should ask her to the Picasso Suite. She does have the keys to the building back there.

Before I can realize this fantasy, my phone beeps. The message says, "Take Martin Luther King Blvd north until it dead ends. Look for Purple Candles. Password at gate is 'Newfoundland.' You're in for a night you'll never forget. Hurry – I'm waiting."

My mouth drops. Is this really happening? I feel like a million bucks in a woman's Coach handbag. I go into the men's room and find the vending machine she's talking about. The instructions say to insert four quarters for a condom, but an "Out of Order" sign glares at me. Just when things are looking up, this happens. I hit the machine. Is there anything in there? I give up after a few pounds and retreat to the front desk worker.

"You covered now?" she asks.

"Actually, the machine in the men's room is busted. Can I ask you a huge favor? Would you check the ladies' room?"

"I can't leave my post or I'll lose my job. That's our policy."

"Alright, I can certainly understand that."

"Just make it quick. You'll be fine," she says.

I go back to the restrooms. It's quiet—no drunken girls stumbling toward the toilet, no guys running to barf, at least not right now. I use my pointer finger to push the door to the ladies' room. As the door squeaks open, the smell of lavender rolls out. Ahh, very nice.

Inside is a space twice the size of the men's room. There's a sitting area with two chairs in front of a vanity mirror. A lavender display is producing the scent. Men get the bare bones—a couple urinals, a few sinks, and a place to throw your towel. They want us in and out. If they put a television or an arcade game in there, maybe we wouldn't have to stand outside waiting for our ladies like dogs waiting for their masters. I'd love to play a game of Pac-Man after relieving myself, or how about *while* relieving myself!

Three stalls are inside, no urinals of course. There's the vending machine attached to the far wall. I sneak toward it and see "Four quarters for a condom." I haven't been condom shopping in a long time, but this seems a tad overpriced. Luckily, I have exact change. As I insert four quarters, a sneeze erupts from the center stall. Oh shit! What should I do?!

I pull the lever.

The toilet flushes.

A condom package falls down. I grab it, but the door to the second stall opens. It's the porcelain girl from the lounge. Wow, she looks good in this light, her skin like the doll my mother used to have on display in our rec room. I liked that doll, not in a sexual way, but—

She shrieks!

I dart out of the room and scurry past the front desk. That scream sounded like it traveled all the way up to the da Vinci Suite.

"I thought you said it'd be fine!" I say to the crooked front desk worker.

I near the exit, but bump into a stealthy man, my height, same parted hair, glasses in my design. He kind of looks like me. Where is he going?

I'm outside now with my valet ticket in hand. It's still damn hot out here. There's Forest Gump talking with normal diction to another valet attendant. He's not retarded!

"You!" I say as he comes my way.

"Hey, your friend gave me money to—"

"Save the explanation," I say, shoving my ticket into his hand.

Forest grabs my keys from the box and runs to the side lot.

My body and my mind have left The Art House. Where am I going? I'm all alone now, no wingman, no friendly in the sky. It's just me and this condom.

Forest races my car around as if a helicopter and three cop cars are chasing him. I hate valet attendants—my poor Scion. That dent on the hood is getting bigger. As I walk around to the driver's side, Forest holds the door open with his hand out.

I start twitching and blinking rapidly. "My…my…my…money is all go…go…gone."

I hop in and put the car into drive. Before hitting the gas, I see that porcelain girl looking at me. She's with one of her friends.

"Aww, I didn't know you're retarded. That's why you were in the women's room," she says through my open passenger side window.

I simply step on the gas and leave this place behind. The ominous black-and-white building trails in my rear-view mirror. It's a place that I never knew existed, a transplant from the East Coast to the West Coast. There were some bizarre creatures inside that place, but my night is just beginning.

# 10

Where do you go when you don't know where to go? I'm driving down the Strip past this building with a space ship on its roof. Is that where they keep the aliens? Am I going north? I'm all turned around in this city. This car needs a compass, but would a compass even know where to go in this city? There's the Treasure Island. A guy in a Hawaiian shirt is taking a picture of two Asian tourists posing in front of the pirate ship. Shit! I gotta ask someone where to go. Jazmin is waiting and my grandmother said never to make a woman wait. If my grandmother could only see me now…

My cell phone rings. It's Javier. He's not going to ruin this!

"Hey, where is Martin Luther King Boulevard?" I ask into the phone.

"Shit, man. They got me! They got me!" Javier shouts.

"What are you talking about? Is this another joke?"

"No, I'm dead serious."

"Who's got you?" I ask.

"These guys. Shit, man. You gotta help me."

"I'm on my way to meet that black chick."

"Screw her!"

"That's exactly what I want to do!" I shout.

"No, man. She can wait. Just come get me."

"What's going on?!"

"Oh shit! They're coming. Take the Strip going away from the Stratosphere. Make a left on Harmon. I'm right by the Hard Rock."

Then the phone goes dead.

"Javier?! Javier?!"

The sound of silence returns. That bastard! He did this to me back in college, and his *just come get me* turned into me racing around town, running stop signs, burning rubber, in order to escape these guys he'd stiffed on his share of beer money. This night is not going to go south! I'm on a roll here and this sexy woman is waiting for me. What am I saying? I don't even know where she is. If I text her, she'll just tell me to forget it. I'm lost. There's nowhere to park to ask for directions, and these tourists are just as lost as I am. It would probably be just as fast to drive to Javier, help him with whatever crap he's gotten himself into, and then have him draw me a map. Javier probably helped erect the walls around this swingers club.

I pass the Flamingo hotel and come up on the Bellagio. A couple walking arm-in-arm is taking in the tranquil water in front of the hotel. Someday that'll be me, taking a girlfriend back to Las Vegas. Someday.

Planet Hollywood towers to my left. The Luxor is coming up in front of me. I'm running out of runway here. Where is this street? As I whisper its name inside the car, the sign for "Harmon" stares at me. I take a left.

The farther I drive away from the Strip, the more I regret listening to Javier. Jazmin is waiting. She's so hot, the way the lights around that bar got lost inside her chocolate skin, the way her scent seduced me. My penis gets hard at the thought of her on top of me, and me on top of her. Then my penis goes soft as I see Javier standing at the corner of a parking lot with a boot around the wheel of his car.

He flags me down. "Over here!" he yells through my open window.

I spin around and see his immobilized car, the boot constricting it like a chastity belt on an ugly wife.

I get out of my car. "What the hell happened? Where's that Asian chick?"

"She lives right over there by UNLV. She invited me up to her apartment and I was on the couch licking her—"

"Come on, man!"

"Well, I had to drive down here to the drugstore to get rubbers. You know, the one time you're out."

"Or the only time."

"Then, I went across the street to that liquor store and when I came back, my car got booted. I tried to negotiate with these guys, but they tell me that I left the parking lot and that since I did, I got this damn boot, and they want three hundred cash to remove it."

"Hey, man. I don't have any money! I can't bail you out on this one."

"I know. I know. Don't worry. I thought of an idea," he says.

"Listen. I got that black girl waiting for me. She's at this swingers club on Martin Luther King Boulevard."

"Oh, shit. Really? I thought that place was only a legend."

"I gotta go. How do I get there?"

"This should take twenty minutes tops, then you can go, man. I just need this one favor. I told that Asian chick I'd be right back. Plus, I need this car to get to work tonight. You see, we take care of this *one* problem, and then all our problems are solved."

"You need to take a logic class."

"Please, man, don't make me beg."

I exhale. "What do I have to do?"

Two black guys roll our way, wearing those little beanie hats and holding boots like the one on Javier's car. What are those hats called?

"Is this the guy?" the skinny one in front asks.

"Yeah, here he is. He'll take care of you," Javier says, a quiver in his voice.

What the hell did he volunteer me to do? These guys look like they eat geeks for breakfast. The skinny one looks about fifty years old. He has a tattoo of a blob on his forearm, a tattoo that has probably morphed into this indistinguishable mess since getting it when he was my age. The guy behind him is chubby, the kind of guy who never talks and only listens. He's holding a key, the key to the boot on Javier's wheel, the key to escaping this situation.

"Are you *sure* this is the guy?" the skinny guy asks Javier again.

"Yeah, he's the best. He's in town tonight from Hollywood."

I've been referred to as *the geek*, *the nerd*, *the kid*, *the dork*, and even *the bum* once by a passerby when I was looking for my contact lens on the ground near a dumpster, but I've never been referred to as *the guy*.

The skinny guy shows me his pearly whites as if he's trying to lure me like a snake does with the rhythm of its tongue. He gives me a fist bump. "What's up, man? I steady tryin' to find an ace like you. I'm Smokin'."

"Your name is Smokin'?" I ask.

"Smokin' from Hoboken."

"This is Benny from Hollywood," Javier says.

"Yeah, uh, I'm Benny from Hollywood," I repeat.

"My girl's right in there," Smokin' says, gesturing toward a warehouse across the street. "We got all the shit ready to go, but the director fuckin' bailed. If I find the motherfucker." His eyes go wide, the snake ready to strike. I hope I never go from *the guy* to *the motherfucker*.

"Benny will take care of you," Javier says.

"We'll call all this even once you work your magic. This way." Smokin' leads us toward the building, the chubby guy staring right through my back.

My cell phone beeps. It's Jazmin. Shit! The message says, "Where are you?"

I reply with "On my way. Had to make a pit stop."

"If you got to be somewhere else, just have your friend pay me the three hundred," Smokin' says.

"No. No. No. Benny is good. Right, Benny?" Javier says.

Beads of sweat cover Javier's brow. What did I get myself into?

"I'm good," I say.

We make it across the street in front of the building. It looks like one of those buildings they show on the news where they find all those severed limbs and heads of gang members. I slow down as the chubby guy pushes me forward.

"Is there a problem?" Smokin' says.

"I just need a minute to discuss this with my friend here," I say.

Javier and I move a few feet away.

"What the hell did you tell them I do?" I shout with a whisper.

"They said they need a director. Someone who has shot music videos. They have this rapper chick wanting to shoot a video tonight."

"I'm not a music video director!"

Smokin' looks at us over the chubby guy's shoulder.

"Keep your voice down," Javier says. "You know how to do that video editing stuff. Plus you took that filmmaking class in college. I remember you telling me all about it."

"We shot videos of pigeons eating popcorn in the park."

"Just pretend they're pigeons."

Two girls holler from the sunroof of a speeding limo. Javier's eyes droop; he's giving me his puppy dog look. Why does this work on me? I thought this only worked on your parents or your spouse.

"Those girls are waiting for us. Please, man. I'll owe you big time."

I exhale and shake my head. This guy, no, this motherfucker, is going to be the end of me.

We walk up to Smokin' and his friend.

"Come on, guys, let's shoot this shit," Smokin' says.

The chubby guy unlocks a gate in the chain-link fence. There're no windows in the building, no lights around it, no life except for the four lost souls knocking on its door. Do you remember when you were a kid and you always wanted to go to the amusement park? Then when your parents took you, you were overwhelmed with the fun rides around you. But there was that one ride you were terrified of, that one ride that your parents tried to persuade you to go on, but you swore that you would never set foot near it. Well, Las Vegas is an amusement park like no other, and I'm about to step into its scariest ride—the haunted house.

"How many videos you shoot?" Smokin' asks.

"Oh, well, after like six or seven you lose count."

"Fo sho. Any brothas I know?"

He means black people, right? I don't know too many black people, but I hope to get to know a lovely black lady tonight at a swingers club to make up for it.

The chubby guy fiddles with the lock to the side door, which is large enough to back in a bus.

"Oh, I did a video for Diddy Dog in Santa Monica and his son Diddy Puppy," I say.

Javier punches me with his eyes. What did I just say?

"What the fuck? I never heard that shit. You sure you mainstream?"

"I'm as *main* as mainstream gets."

"I don't know what that means, but you'd better make my girl look da shit."

Then the belly of the beast opens. My eyes take in a large room that can fit not one bus, but a half-dozen. Gutted slot machines line the walls with busted neon signs piled across the breadth of the floor. The letters "UNES" are all that are left from one sign. The shards of glass and rusted scrap metal are the same as on the poster asking you, "When was your last tetanus shot?" Beyond that are only shadows.

As we enter, the smell of gasoline hits me. I wish I had my dad's hand to hold as I enter the scariest ride in the amusement park, but my dad is asleep thousands of miles away.

Smokin' sets the boots down in a pile and leads us toward a side office area. An old man, easily seventy years old, is sitting on a stained couch and staring at the snowy picture of a man fishing on a 13" television. The old man has white hair and a white beard. He doesn't even look at us when we enter. Is he the guy they told to shoot a music video forty years ago?!

"Don't worry about him. He's the *caretaka*," Smokin' goes.

"All Benny needs is the equipment and the talent," Javier says.

Smokin' goes into a side room as the chubby guy stands in the corner, watching us.

"Why didn't you just say *you* were the director?" I ask Javier.

"It's all just talk and shouting, right? You know this stuff, I don't."

"I wish I had a computer."

"What's a computer going to do?" Javier says.

"I need to Google how to shoot a rap video."

"Let's just fake it till we make it out of here."

We both stare at the key in the chubby guy's hand. Suddenly, the door opens and out walks a thick black woman, wearing a T-shirt with the word *Thug* written across it. Her hair has a gel-hardened wave in the front and she has a call center microphone protruding from her ear, the cable running down the front of her shirt.

"*This* is the guy?" she says, sizing me up.

"Yeah, so they say," Smokin' replies.

"This is Benny from Hollywood. He'll make you a star," Javier says.

Smokin' wheels in a high-end camera on a tripod and dolly. The thing is easily two-feet long, a professional-looking one at my guess. There are more switches and buttons than inside a cockpit.

"Wow, that's a big black one," I say. Wait a second... That didn't come out right. I try, "Where did you get it?"

Smokin' looks at me, stone-faced.

"Okay, I won't ask any more questions," I chuckle.

"Good idea," Javier says.

On the camera, there are buttons for white balance and manual focus and iris. I'm trying to think back to my class. Where is the auto mode? I should look for the power button first.

"I thought you know how to use that thing," Smokin' says.

"Oh, yeah, I know. This is just the newer model than the one I normally use." My right eye starts twitching.

"Because I don't know that technical shit. You'd better not fuck this up," Smokin' says.

I flip out the viewfinder and press some buttons. Javier reaches in and points at the on/off switch. I slide it; the camera beeps. “Here we go. All good now,” I say.

Smokin’ comes over and points at the closed lens cover.

“Oh, I knew that.” I find the slider to open it. “It’s all good.”

“Whatcha think? Out there, right?” he says.

“Yeah. Let’s put her out there and have her sing the song. I can do some cool camera movements.”

“Well, first of all, she’s rappin’, not *singin’ a fuckin’ song*. And I got the music queued up on the sound system. This’ll help her through it. I got a guy downtown who can video edit this shit. He’s got a fuckin’ fast computer.”

“Oh, hopefully it has at least four gigs of ram. It’s important for editing large files.”

“Not now,” Javier whispers.

I swallow. Javier is right. Let’s just fake this until we make it out of here.

“Alright. Let’s have you out there and then we can bust this *sucka* out,” I say.

The chubby guy squints his eyes.

“Don’t try to sound black; it’s not helping,” Javier mutters.

We go out on the floor, leaving the old man on his couch. Is he even alive?

“How about over there?” I say. She moves in front of the busted signs.

The chubby guy watches from the back.

“If we can just grab that key,” Javier whispers.

“*We*? Try *you*.”

The smell of something burning swirls around me. What is that? Wait. That's the same smell from college every time I'd go to the door of our neighbor to ask him to turn down his Bob Marley music. Then I see the source and know why they call this guy *Smokin'*.

"Want some?" he says, exhaling his burning joint my way.

"No, thanks. I don't have glaucoma."

The rapper chick hums a little voice exercise. I size her up in the camera viewfinder, but she's barely visible.

"You have any lights?" I ask.

"You want lights? I gotch yo lights," Smokin' says. He connects two cables together like Doc Brown on top of the clock tower in *Back to the Future*. A bank of lights ignites, and then another after another. The place lights up. This does look like a cool scene to shoot a rap video.

I center her in the viewfinder.

"Okay. Sound!" I shout.

Music pours from the rafters. It sounds like a kid banging on a synthesizer.

"Camera rolling!" I shout, pressing the record button.

Javier winks at me.

"Action!" I yell.

She bounces around and points at the camera, her eyes wide, her teeth reflecting the light. I move the camera while zooming in and out.

"*I'm a bitch. I'm not yo bitch. I'm not his bitch. I'm not her bitch. I'm…*" She stops and bites her lip. Her voice is up and down like the rollercoaster at Hersheypark.

"It's okay, girl." Smokin' looks at me. "Whatcha think?"

"She's great," I lie.

Javier stares at me. I give him the same eyes I gave him after telling a girl he'd introduced me to that I was majoring in lovemaking and she was the final exam. She poured her drink over my head.

"It's okay. The editor can pick and choose the good parts. Let's shoot it from the top again," I say.

The rapper chick hops and makes monkey sounds. Is this what all the rappers do before hitting the record button?

"Sound!" I shout.

Smokin' puts the track back to the beginning.

"Camera rolling! And… Action!"

She does her thing as I zoom, move, and pan. This is kinda fun. I can be a director. She finishes her two-minute rap, which is filled with more bitches than the backyard at a dog breeding business.

Smokin' starts clapping. "That's my girl. Isn't she da shit?"

"She's the *shit* alright," I mutter to Javier.

"Shh… Hey, bring us all in the back. I have a plan," he whispers.

Javier having a plan is like a baby having a dirty diaper. Actually, having a dirty diaper right now might get us out of this situation.

"What's in the back there?" I ask.

"Oh, you'll like that shit," Smokin' says, leading us through the shadows.

Dust chokes me as we move down a concrete passage. This is a bad idea, but I guess if I'm going to be killed, I'd rather not see it coming.

"Hey, grab that light, yo," Smokin' says to Javier.

As we travel into the bowels of the building, Javier shines the light, revealing a vast area looking like New York City. There are murals of buildings and alleyways with the authentic touch of graffiti.

"Wow, this is awesome! How did you find this place? Do you guys have a permit to shoot here?"

"Permit? I got my permit right here." Smokin' pulls out a pistol from the back of his waistband.

My heart stops. I can't breathe. Javier had better have a good plan, but when I look at him, he crosses himself as if we're in a church. That's the first and probably the last time I've ever seen him do that.

"Lights. We need a lot of lights here. Right, Benny?" Javier goes.

I squint my eyes at him.

"*Right*, Benny?" he repeats.

This must be part of his plan. "Yeah. You're right. You're my DP on this one. Let's get the lights."

Javier snakes the cord into the room. He brings it around the chubby guy and positions one of the floodlights on the ground.

"Is that working?" he asks Smokin', referencing another floodlight with a long cord.

Smokin' nods, puffing more smoke. My head feels light. Am I getting a contact high?

Javier plugs the light in, bringing the cord around Smokin's feet in order to position the light from the other angle.

Under different circumstances, this would be a cool setting to shoot a video. This room looks like an NYC alleyway inside the viewfinder. Javier finishes positioning the lights. Is he trying to blind them? What the hell is he doing? I don't want to be shot. Would he take a bullet for me? No, he'd probably want me to take the bullet and then offer to pay my estate back in cheap beer.

He's clutching the cords tightly in his hand. Hmm. What are you doing, Javier?

My phone beeps again. It's another message from Jazmin, "Your time is almost up…"

Shit! I can't blow this; I won't blow this! I have to go. My heart is ready to pound out of my chest. I reply with, "Almost there."

"I'm ready, Benny," Javier says.

"Just do this one without music," I say. "You're the best. This is going to be *da shit*—I mean great."

She nods.

"Okay, girl. Show me whatcha got," Smokin' goes.

The chubby guy is staring at us. Does he know what we're about to do? I don't even know what we're about to do.

"Lights! … Camera! … Action!"

Javier yanks the cords. The slack tightens around the feet of Smokin' and the chubby guy. Both go down, constricted by the snake.

"Run!" Javier yells.

I take off as Javier snatches the key on the ground. I run faster than even that time a ten-year-old chased me because she thought I'd stolen her candy.

Two gunshots echo through the building. Are they shooting at us?!

"Shit! Move!" I shout.

Javier and I make it back to the open room. Glass crunches under our shoes as we bolt toward the doorway. Suddenly, the old man stands up and watches us go. He *is* alive and so are we!

"Get out while you have the chance," he says.

I nod at him as we share a stare for a split second, and during this time, I can see myself in his eyes forty years from now—old, gray, wrinkled.

Javier and I make it out onto the street into the desert heat. The old man, the *caretaka*, pulls the door closed, sealing in the chaos. As we dash across the street, Javier starts huffing next to me. I've never heard him out of breath before, but then again, three years can change a man for the better or for the worse.

We reach the cars.

Javier pops off the boot using the key. "I'm sorry, Benny."

"It's not *Benny*."

"I know."

I fire up my Scion.

"To get to Martin Luther King Boulevard, head straight down Harmon, and then make a right onto Industrial," he says. "Now go get that girl. I owe you one."

"Ahh," I exhale, looking him in the eye, seeing the Benjamin from college reflecting back. "Don't worry about it. Just be safe," I say.

He clenches his fist and gives me a shadow punch. Javier is going to be the end of me, but I pray it occurs only after I meet the woman from my dreams.

# 11

The roads in Vegas are lonely. There are just as many cabs on the roads as lights in the casinos. As I drive down Industrial Road, the seedy side of Vegas surrounds me. A windowless building with blue lights pulls on the cones in my eyes. The sign out front says, "Sapphire." There are train tracks running parallel to me. Where do they lead?

I'm lost in the enigma of night. A Rolls-Royce in front of me has "WYNN 2" on its license plate. Up ahead is a place called, "Hushh The Club." A man wearing a coat is lying on the sidewalk out front. It's ninety degrees out here. Why does he need a coat?

Down a side road is massage parlor after massage parlor. Some say thirty dollars for a half-hour massage; one says twenty-nine. They all have black windows with the proverbial "Open" sign flashing. I suppose I could always go there, but the thought of the pain my bones would have to endure to get to the happy part keeps me focused on the road ahead. Where is this place? I'm not going to find it this way.

I pull over into a gas station. Five black men in their thirties are laughing outside the store.

"Excuse me," I say to them through my open window.

The men look at me. They are big with tattoos.

"Is Martin Luther King up this way?" I ask, glancing at my phone.

They fan out, their expressions turn from smiles to scowls. The biggest guy in front steps toward me. Is that a tattoo of a gun?

"Martin Luther King? Is that some kind of joke?" he says.

"Yeah, you're a long way from the country club, Bill Gates," another one says.

What are they talking about? I just want directions. Oh shit! I forgot to say the type of road. I just simplified it for brevity's sake, but I don't think these guys know what *brevity* means.

"No, Martin Luther King *Boulevard*," I clarify, but it's too late.

"Why don't you get out and we'll show you?" the one with the gun tattoo says.

They start pounding on my car as my body shakes. The guy with the gun tattoo punches the hood. I punch the gas as my rear window blows out. Glass flies everywhere. I duck as I speed out of the parking lot.

"Jesus Christ!" I yell. "My car!"

I drive for miles, turning left on a four-lane road, making a right on a side street. All I want to do is drive. I pass more offbeat casinos and even more massage parlors. Ten minutes go by before my breathing returns to normal. My car is hot, the night air breaching my sanctuary through the rear window. How am I going to pay for this damage? Does insurance cover getting assaulted in Vegas? Will my agent believe me?

The traffic light in front of me turns red, so I stop. Overhead, the street sign says, "Cheyenne." Should I keep going? Should I go home? Jazmin floats to the front of my mind; she pacifies me, excites me, fixes the dents on my car. How am I going to find her?

A pink Cadillac pulls up alongside me. It's a 1950s model, a convertible. Elvis is driving. Perhaps Elvis is going to the same place.

"Excuse me, where is the *street* named Martin Luther King?"

He looks over. He's the fat Elvis, the one from the '70s, not the '50s army man or the '60s leading actor. He's wearing sunglasses even though it's pitch black out here. How can he see?

"Take a right, two blocks up, uh-huh huh!"

The light turns green and he is still looking at me when he hits the gas. I watch him speed into the night. That's a nice ride.

As I follow Elvis' directions, I text Jazmin: "Sorry. I really am almost there. Promise."

The elusive boulevard named after the prominent black leader is finally before me. This is it. I take this road to the end. Homes with barrel roofs and abandoned cars scatter the street. The lights of Vegas, the lights of life, are behind me. Where are the purple candles from her text message? Are they supposed to be purple lights, pictures of purple flames, or two blazing torches? How can fire be purple?

I'm driving past half-built houses and desert lots. A dog runs out in front of my car, so I slam on the brakes. The broken glass slides around in the back. Where am I going? I'm a sitting duck out here. Anyone, anything, can enter my back window. I should turn around, go back to Javier's apartment, and get some sleep.

But then, I see it—a massive mansion surrounded by a ten-foot wrought-iron fence. Gargoyles are perched on the gate with two subtle yet distinct candles flickering in purple. They found a way to make fire burn purple. Perhaps the flame is hotter than hell.

A tall man in a suit is standing at the gate, so I pull up and lower my window. He looks like my cousin in New York, a Wall Street stockbroker with a pudgy face and a receding hairline. However, as he approaches, his eyes say he's not my cousin; he's someone with a secret.

"Good evening, sir. May I help you?" the gatekeeper says.

"Uh, I'm meeting someone in there," I reply.

He takes a step back, his shoes clinking on the macadam, and looks at my busted window and at the dents on my hood. "Are you sure you know where you are going, sir?" he says.

Oh, yeah. Isn't there a password? "Oh, wait. I have something for you." I flip through my phone. "Newfoundland," I say.

"Very well, sir," he says with a smirk that I've seen before on Javier's face.

"So, does the password change to a different island each night?" I ask.

"Newfoundland. It's not the island; it's the dog breed." The gatekeeper walks over and presses a button; the gate squeaks open.

The mansion towers in front of me. "So what do I do?"

He chuckles as he waves his hand. "I'm not the person to ask. I hope you find *who* or *what* you're looking for."

He can't help me anymore. This is all me now. Do I really want to go through with this? What if it's some elaborate plot to steal my car or my identity? Jazmin did get a text message during our conversation. I'm thinking too much. It's only sex, right?

As my mind races, I'm already past the gate and heading into the unknown. The tires on my car crunch on the gravelly ground. A groomed desert landscape surrounds me with cacti and unique rocks. The mansion has at least twenty windows lining the front with subtle lights filling a few. Jaguars, BMWs, Cadillacs, and Lexi are parked around the entryway. There're no swings; they must be inside.

A gray-haired doorman is standing guard at the doorway, watching me park. The man looks like the uncle of the guy at the gate. I park next to a new Porsche 911 Carrera S. Maybe it's Jazmin's car.

As I turn off the engine, the sound of silence surrounds me. A bird squawks somewhere in the distance. What am I doing?

Gravel crunches behind me. Is someone there?

Only the shadows of the cacti loiter. As I take a gulp, my throat clenches. Really, what am I doing?

I put my cell phone in my pocket and check my wallet. My work I.D. is intact and my condom is ready like a sterile glove for a brain surgeon. Okay, you can do this. This is going to be fun. Jazmin is waiting.

I lick my lips and lower the vanity mirror. There he is, Benjamin Pollock. Remember, you are suave, cool, a Vegas player. This place is your regular hangout. You'll walk in there with your head up, your eyes open, and your stride long. You'll find Jazmin, whisk her away, and bed her.

I step out of the car. It's useless to lock it with a hole the size of the Grand Canyon in the back. I roll up my sleeves as I walk through the night. The air has gotten cooler and it flows through my collar and enters my pores.

The entryway has a door sturdy enough to keep out unwanted visitors…or keep them in. It's so big that it requires a special man to open it, and this special man is watching to see if this visitor is wanted.

"Welcome. Where is your date?" he says.

"She's inside."

"If you don't find her, I'm sure there will be an alternative." He removes a cigarette from his suit jacket. This guy reminds me of a politician, but he's not wearing a lapel pin on his jacket. "Hey, you got a light?"

"I don't smoke…" I reply. Wait. What about my excursion at The Art House, the parting gift that should still be in my pocket? There it is. I strike the match and offer the man some fire. Offering fire for a smoke is like offering ice for a drink, except it doesn't melt; it only burns you.

"Thanks," he says.

The matchbook has numbers written inside it. They look like IP addresses to computers. One of these numbers is familiar. No. They're probably just random, but someone wrote them. Who? Why?

The doorman does his job. "Here you go. Enjoy."

I put the matchbook into my wallet and look into the structure. It's dark in there, darker than the outside. "Thank you, sir," I say, entering.

Inside, candles are flickering down a hallway with cheetah-print carpet leading somewhere. A woman in a red dress is standing behind a cash register—the toll keeper. Why do you have to pay to get in here? And how much is it?

"Hello, young man. We generally don't allow single men in alone," she says.

"Well, I'm supposed to be meeting someone."

"Your name?" she asks.

"Benjamin."

The woman scans a list. Her hair is long, straight, with a perfect part in the middle. I always have a hard time with my part. She has a book open in front of her. It looks like a novel.

"I don't see a *Benjamin*," she says.

No Benjamin? Jazmin has my name, right? I'm positive I gave it to her. Did she forget it? Or maybe this is just a sick joke. I should turn around and go home, not to Javier's place, but to my home in LA. I can still make it before sunrise. Then, I can flush this night down the toilet. However, Jazmin had said that she liked me. Her black skin had brushed against me; her scent of sexiness had seduced me. What else could the name be under?

"Uh, check under Bill G," I say.

She looks again. "Here you are," she says. "Looks like your acquaintance provided us with a coupon."

"A coupon? Where do you get a coupon for a place like this? Do they print them in the Sunday papers out here?"

She chuckles and winks. "Tonight must be your lucky night. It'll be thirty dollars instead of the usual fifty."

That's a large fee, coupon or not. You have to pay to play in Vegas. I give her two twenties, the last two twenties I have. She takes a pen next to the register and marks both bills, studying the lines to check for counterfeits. What does she think? Whoever uses counterfeit bills to pay admission to a swingers club should be banned from ever having sex again. It's an insult when a clerk checks your money. When she gives me a ten for change, I grab the pen and check the bill.

"This should work both ways," I say.

She smiles and shrugs. "Well, maybe you should take that pen inside with you to check for counterfeits."

All I can do is smile. This lady in red is coy. From my guess, she looks about forty. Maybe I should ask her out, but then she lifts up the book. It's not a novel; it's a nonfiction book—"How to Kill a MAN and Get Away with It..." I swallow hard and go toward the heart of the house.

The hallway is long. It smells like Pledge in here; it smells like my grandmother's house. Animals are everywhere. A life-size deer greets me. A glass case with foxes frozen in a scamper is on display. Bison heads guard the doorways down the hall. This is not my grandmother's house.

Suddenly, I hear the sound of panting. It's definitely a woman. Is she in pain? Is she being operated on? I stop cold. It sounds like it's coming from a room with an open door. As I move toward it, the panting changes to moaning.

Inside, shadows distort my view. My eyes adjust to the hourglass silhouettes of two figures. Wait. Their backsides are exposed! Another woman is bouncing up and down on something…or rather, someone! The woman whimpers. She's the source of the sounds. This is *definitely* not my grandmother's house! The sight alone is enough to arouse me, but what really sets me off is the fact that the door is wide open. It's not cracked an inch, or halfway closed; it's open for a reason.

"You shouldn't hide that thing."

Jazmin is standing in a bikini. Her chocolate skin electrifies my eyes. A red top hides her bulging breasts and a red thong makes me go crazy. I finally look at her eyes and see they're fixed on my erection.

I cover my bulge and laugh. Women have it easy. How can we tell whether a woman is aroused? Some say it's hidden in her nipples or her body language. I never had that gift of detection, but I suppose that's why I had to drive all this way into the darkness. "Jazmin. Wow, you look great."

She comes my way. She's taller than I thought. I'm 6'2", but I'm all geek. She's 6'2", but she's all goddess. As soon as she nears me, I can taste her sexiness.

She caresses my shirt. "I'm glad you *finally* made it."

"I'm sorry. I got lost inside New York City."

"I was this close to leaving." She shows me an inch gap between her thumb and her pointer finger. "But you're lucky I didn't because I have a surprise for you. You want a tour first?"

"Well…sure."

Getting a tour of a swingers club is bizarre enough, but getting one from a hot woman in a bikini should only be reserved for a special occasion.

Jazmin grabs my hand. It's hot, damn hot. She leads me further into the obscurities. We enter a huge room that looks like a pool hall with a half-dozen tables offering a game of sink-the-ball. However, these are not pool tables; they are queen-size beds. I guess they are still good for a game of sink-the-ball.

We move toward a small bar. A thirty-something bartender is standing at his post in front of a wall of alcohol bottles. He looks foreign, maybe Indian or Israeli. The weird thing is that he looks at me first, instead of my tour guide.

"The bar," Jazmin says.

The bartender gives me a nod of acceptance.

We continue toward the sound of music. It's techno with a hypnotic vibe. Inside a room, lights are dancing alongside a couple in swimwear. A DJ is bobbing his head with one side of headphones against his ear. He's staring at an Apple laptop. Is he implementing some security patches for the house's computer network?

Jazmin squeezes my hand. She starts gyrating around me, grinding her ass into my groin. I take her hand and move with her. The last time that I danced was at the company holiday party, but I don't remember them playing this song.

I try to move to the rhythm, but my hips don't respond. I'm out of shape. I wish I could dance better. It's funny how humans are the only species who dance. You never see animals dance when music comes on. Why is that?

I do a little spin. The couple in swimwear laughs. Who cares? All I care about is Jazmin. I'll do whatever she wants me to do.

"I can see some potential," she says.

"Just you wait," I say, taking her hand and spinning her. I step on her heels; she bobbles, and then falls into me, causing us both to go down to the floor. The music stops. Oops.

"Sorry. We're okay," I say, picking us both up.

A sudden urge comes over me. "Wait right here," I say to Jazmin.

I scurry to the DJ to ask him whether he has a song that I danced to in high school, a song that I spent weeks and weeks memorizing for our school talent show. We won that year.

The music changes to Michael Jackson's "Beat It." A few more people in swimwear enter. Oh, no, I can handle an audience of four, but that's it. Jazmin is smiling, and I mean her cleavage.

Come on, Benjamin. Just do this like in high school. You remember the steps. I slide to the middle of the dance floor. It's only me out here.

The beat starts. I move my hips, sway left, and then right.

Jazmin is laughing and moving her head.

I reach above my head and move left, and then reach again and move right. I repeat the steps, kicking, sliding, letting the music manipulate my muscles. Then I let it all out, gliding in the moonwalk. I still remember it after all these years. I twirl and grab my crotch. "*Oohhhhh*!"

Then I collapse on the ground with a smile on my face. The scantily dressed crowd cheers. A woman claps her breasts together. What the fuck?!

Jazmin leads the cheers as she helps me up. "I never knew computer geeks could dance," she says.

"You should see my 'Thriller.'"

"Let's go outside," she says.

"What's outside?"

Jazmin scurries toward a set of double doors. The DJ changes the music back to techno and gives me the thumbs-up. Remember how everyone used to ask you what you wanted to be as a kid—you know, your grandmother and your aunts and uncles? I used to say that I wanted to be a DJ.

Jazmin pulls me outside. Girls are giggling and water is splashing. I'm at the pool. There are twenty bodies enjoying the water with beer bottles and wine glasses surrounding them on tables.

"Hey, everyone, I've got fresh meat," Jazmin announces.

The group turns and swims to the edge, the water distorting their bodies. Are they all naked?

"He looks yummy! Off with his clothes!" a busty blonde says.

Jazmin tugs my shirt, actually Javier's shirt. Where the hell is he right now?

"Let's take a dip before we..." she starts to say, and then finishes by batting her eyes.

When I was eight-years-old at summer camp, one of the counselors threw me into the water. I almost drowned because of those evil camp counselors. And here, now swimming naked... Hell no! "Uh, well, you can go in," I say.

"I want to get you wet," she whispers.

Like a curious tortoise, another erection starts poking my pants. "I can't swim," I reveal.

Jazmin frowns. She unfastens her heels, removes her bikini top, and then steps out of her bottoms. Her breasts are large and in charge. They are firm and full, surely a C-cup, maybe even a D. She has these perfect red nipples that are winking at me. Her flat tummy leads down to her shaved kitty.

It's so clean, the pool lights reflecting off it. Beggars can't be choosers, but I like a clean kitty. Why do women have hair there anyway? Is it to mask their most precious spot? I suspect it's to prevent germs from entering, a trait inherited from the caveman days, and I guess today, it still does prevent germs from entering—germs named *horny men.*

Jazmin hands me her bikini, and then runs toward the pool. Her feminine frame soars through the air, and then plunges into the water.

I kneel down near the edge and touch the water. "Feels warm," I say.

Jazmin swims over to me with her breasts floating on the water. Does that mean they're real or fake? "Why won't you get in here? Are you afraid of me?"

"Ha! Well, I usually don't play water polo in the buff."

The busty blonde swims over and splashes me. "No clothes allowed out here. I can see that turtle of yours wanting to come out, so let him out."

The eyes of the drunken swimmers see through my clothes, see the real Benjamin. I'm a piece of meat out here, a meal for the hungry sharks.

"I need a drink," I say as I set down Jazmin's bikini.

I retreat into the house, the naked people hooting and hollering. Where is that bar? A naked man and woman are walking toward the pool. My erection still sings. Erections are like two-year-olds; they fidget, cry, and throw a tantrum when you want them to sleep.

"Nice moves back there," the naked man says.

"Thanks."

Around an elephant tusk on display, I find the bar. There's that bartender.

"How come you're not outside?" he goes.

"How come *you're* not outside?" I counter.

He must be Greek. That's it. I've heard that accent before at my great uncle's funeral. He had a bunch of Greek friends.

"What are you having?" he asks.

The wall of liquor towers in front of me. There's one of everything except there're three bottles of "Jack Daniel's Old Tennessee Whiskey."

"Corona," I say.

"*La cerveza más fina.* Good choice," he replies.

Maybe he's Hispanic. I can't tell. I can never really tell.

He grabs a frosty bottle from a refrigerator chest, pops off the top, and stuffs a lime down its throat.

"My old college roommate hooked me on it."

Giggles come from two fetching females wearing red silk robes. They stop at the far end of the bar and kiss like there's no tomorrow.

"Thanks," I say as I take a long gulp. The alcohol coats my belly. "What do I owe ya?"

"We have an open bar. Part of your fee," he replies.

"Wow, nice. I might need a case of this before the night's over."

He looks at the wall and I follow his gaze to the clock. It's 1:55 in the morning.

"Well, you got about four hours before sunrise."

By my calculation, I'll enjoy a nice drink for a few minutes, and then Jazmin will come in, and then I can take care of her for twenty minutes (I hope it's at least twenty minutes!), and then I can call it a night. Yes. This night is going good. The two girls start moaning next to us. No, this night is going great!

"How do you handle this job?" I ask the bartender.

"Ha, I ask myself that every night, bro. It's really about eye contact. I take it this is your first time."

"Yeah, I think I'm in over my head," I say, taking another drink.

"What do you do?"

"I'm an Information Systems Policy Analyst."

"In Vegas?"

"LA."

"You're a long way from home. How did you find this place?" he asks.

That question is worth a million bucks. The pool people are laughing loudly. "This place found me."

"Hey, I've got a question for ya. This computer is randomly rebooting back here. Maybe you can check it out."

He points at a Dell OptiPlex, a decent business computer designed for tight spaces and always-on functionality. "Well…sure, I guess."

I step around the girls. One is kissing the other's breast. Bizarrely, the sight doesn't faze me. I guess I'm a one-woman kind of guy, and my woman is outside, getting wet.

There's a 17" flat-screen sitting on top of the computer case. The Dell is running Windows XP. I check the task manager and see that it still has over 60% of its memory free. There's not much running in the system tray.

As I look at the hardware, the girls reflect back inside a bottle of gin, but I only see one of them. Oh, the other one is kneeling. Oh my! I trace the keyboard and mouse around the back. There're a lot of cables. I move the monitor off the top and open the case. Wires are everywhere. There're no bulging capacitors. Oh, there we go. "Hmm, I think I see the problem. Yes."

"Yes! Oh, yes!" one of the girls yells.

I reach my hand deep inside the computer.

"Yes! Deeper!" the girl screams.

I fiddle with the fan wires.

"Right there! Right there!" she yells.

I plug the wire into its spot; the fan spins up.

"Ohhh!" the girl exhales. "You found my spot."

"Here's your problem," I say. "The computer is overheating. Fan header number one on your motherboard died. I plugged your fan into number two." I remove a Post-it note blocking the outside of the exhaust port. "Plus, you had this Post-it note blocking the exhaust vent."

"Hey, you're alright, bro!"

The two women slide into the next room.

"What were they saying?" I ask, reassembling the computer.

"I think they liked how you fix a computer," he chuckles.

"I wonder how my date is doing," I say, returning to my drink.

"Oh… *Her*," he goes, raising his thick eyebrows.

Don't tell me she's a man. She can't be a man. I saw her completely naked. She's definitely not a man. That's all that I care about. "What about her? Should I wear two condoms?"

"Well, just be careful. That's all."

"Come on. What is it?" I say.

"Just remember, even the best garden has a weed, sometimes a big weed."

"What do you mean?" I reply. Don't talk in code. I need cold, hard facts right now. Weeds? Gardens? She must have an STD. Shit! I can't get an STD. But she's so hot.

"There you are," Jazmin says.

My eyes go wide.

The bartender winks at me. "Good luck."

What does he mean? Is a wink good or bad? I just fixed this guy's computer. He owes me. If there's something really bad, he should tell me—he must! Maybe it's not that bad.

Jazmin is wearing a fluffy white robe. It's open a few inches, giving me a view of the delicate skin between her breasts. She has a twinkle in her eye and she tells me to "come here" with her finger. I'm going for it!

"How was the pool?" I ask, taking a swig of my beer.

She hooks me and kisses me deeply, sucking the beer from my mouth. What should I do?! Go ahead, take it. Whoa, there's her tongue probing my mouth. I try to match her vigor, but I can't. Finally, she relinquishes and whispers into my ear, "I'm all wet now."

My penis is throbbing. I want this woman here and now. The open room is adjacent to us with those two fetching females. They have their robes off and are now rolling around on one of the queen-size beds.

"Let's find some place to play," Jazmin says.

She takes my hand and brings me to a room with a pool table. So this house does have a place to play a round of billiards. Two guys are hitting balls while their ladies are watching and puffing cigars. There's a leather couch against the wall.

"Hmm, I'd like to pocket some balls in there," she says.

"I don't know, you might scratch," I reply.

"Why? Does your pool stick need some chalking?"

"No, I just don't broadcast my game," I say, trying to be tactful. She might want to put on a show for the house. Maybe that's what gives her some kicks, but there's no way I'm going to strip naked in front of others, not even if there's a naked black woman next to me. Well…

"Let's see what's over here," she says.

We move to a room across the hall. Leopard-print sheets cover a queen-size bed. I always pictured doing it on leopard print. It's every teenage boy's fantasy to do it like a porn star in a staged room. I take a drink of my beer and feel the alcohol kicking inside my veins. It's screaming through my engorged penis.

Sex grounds you. It makes you forget your worries, your stresses, your boring life; it gives your life meaning. It gives you a clear objective in an unclear world. All I care about is right here, right now; all I care about is Jazmin.

"Now, this is more like it," I say, eyeing myself in the mirror in the corner. Reflecting back, there's no computer geek, no introverted loner, no boring boy without balls; there's only a man.

"Take off those preppy clothes," she says.

I remove the things in my pocket and set them on the nightstand. Jazmin fixes her hair in the mirror. Getting laid has been my goal, but having an exotic model, a kinky Vegas girl, a lioness, excites me. I'm a lucky man. However, as I lay my wallet on the nightstand, I remember the warning from the bartender and that wink he gave me. Hmm. Well, my condom is still in its place. This should eliminate all of my concerns.

"And I came prepared," I say.

"Only one?"

"What do you have in mind?"

"You'll see," she says, winking.

My fingers twitch. This woman is full of surprises. I unbutton my shirt as she nears me. Breathing her sexy scent makes my toes curl. Is this really happening?

"I'll be right back. I need to freshen up," she whispers. Then she leaves the room, shutting the door.

I kick off my pants. I'm standing in my boxers. They're white, sterile, but a ring of pre-cum saturates the cotton.

"Don't let me down, boy," I say to my penis.

I go to the mirror and flex my muscles. I need to work out. I jump, flap my arms, and loosen up. Should I stand or sit? Take my boxers off or leave them on? I sit down and leave them on. I'll let her take them off. Wow, my heart is really pounding.

Think back to the last time you had sex. Do you remember what *you* were doing before you started Act One? I bet you don't. This moment will probably never be stored in my brain. I'll remember the act of sex forever, but not these minutes of time. They will be lost. These types of moments happen all the time; they happen more than we think. But if we live through these moments and our brains fail to record them, did they still happen?

The door creaks open and I sit up. The condom wrapper sparkles on the table next to me. I'm ready. A shadow shifts at the door, a large shadow. My eyes open wide as my heart suddenly stops.

A morbidly obese black woman enters the room. Her body is so large that she waddles when she moves. A bra is hiding breasts the size of watermelons during a rainy summer. Is she even wearing panties? Rolls of fat are hanging down from her belly.

Hidden behind her is Jazmin. "This is Peaches," she says.

The fat woman smiles, her eyes studying me.

"Peaches?" I say. "I'm afraid to ask why they call you that."

"I'm as juicy as a Peach. I hear you have some huckleberries for me," she says, her voice as deep as the voice of James Earl Jones.

Jazmin shuts the door, sealing the three of us inside. My muscles lock. I'm too afraid to run, too afraid to scream. Jazmin stands next to her, a before-and-after body during a season on *The Biggest Loser*.

"You have a choice. I know you want me, but you must service Peaches first, and I want to watch."

Two women are in front of me. A robe is covering Jazmin's tall frame, but next to her, fat is covering Peaches' wide frame. My penis shrivels up to a prune. I need to get out of here. The door is behind Peaches, so how can I escape? Going around won't work. Is there a way under her? There's no way I'm going between her legs. Can I go above her? Maybe I can jump on the bed and flip over her body. For sure she can't jump, but I can't either. I'm trapped. So *this* is what the bartender meant.

"You're not goin' nowhere," Peaches growls as she sees me looking for my escape route.

Just pretend this is a video game and Peaches is the final boss. I can beat her. I've played a lot of video games.

I channel all of my energy and in a flash, I grab my clothes and run.

Peaches tosses me back on the bed as my clothes fly from my hands. The bed has cushioned my fall, but I'm lying on my back. Peaches soars in the air. I try to move, try to react, but I can't. All I can do is watch her body do a belly flop into the pool, and I'm the pool! Her weight crushes my bones. My lungs collapse. I can't breathe! Peaches starts licking my face like a dog licking its owner after a long day at work. Is this the end? I hope my parents don't cry too much when they read my obituary: *Computer Geek Crushed by Tractor Trailer in Las Vegas*.

I have to do something! "Okay! Okay!" I wheeze.

Peaches lets up her grasp. She rolls off me as I fill my lungs with air.

"You're a whole lot of woman," I say.

Jazmin joins us on the bed. The mattress springs cry from the weight. I swallow hard. I can do this. If I service Peaches, I can have Jazmin. Just block Peaches out, make it one of those memories that doesn't get stored.

"Why don't you, uh, get on your back? It'll be easier that way," I say.

Peaches lies back. When she raises her arms, the stench of sweat stings me. How long has that been hidden under there? I nearly gag, but then Jazmin's sexy scent brings me back. It's a cocktail of odor, an upper and a downer. My body doesn't know whether to flee or to fuck.

I glance at the door, but then Jazmin looks at me and shakes her head. I'm going to have to go through with this. I slide down the bed, passing a mole on Peaches' naval with thick hair growing out of it. I'm at her knees now, looking between her legs. The smell of more sweat hits me. Oh God, this is disgusting. How am I going to do this?

"Uh, I need some pillows," I say, gesturing to some on the couch in the corner of the room.

Jazmin squints her eyes, trying to read me. I go to stand up.

"You stay here and I'll get them," she says, going to the couch.

"Come here, you," Peaches says.

She squeezes her legs together. She has me around the neck with my head at her knees. She's cutting off the blood supply to my brain! I try to wriggle my way free. The stubble on her legs scratches my face. I spread her legs open, and then slide out.

I'm free!

"Get back here!" Peaches yells.

I bolt out of the room, a free man covered only by his boxers. I run down the hallway toward the front door. Oh shit! This is the wrong way. I turn, but Jazmin is standing guard. "Hey!" she yells.

Peaches erupts from the door. "Get back here, my love!"

That way is not going to work. I run deeper into the belly of the mansion. Those two fetching females are still going at it, now doing a 69. Wow! Look at them. That one's tongue is—

"We aren't through with you yet!" Jazmin yells.

Godzilla is stomping my way. I keep going. There's the bartender serving someone, but at the sight of me, he widens his eyes and pours the liquor over the edge of the glass.

"You should have warned me!" I shout to him.

I run outside toward the pool with the crazed crowd. As if a swarm of angry bees is chasing me, I dive into the pool. The water pelts my face. I go down deep and see penises flapping and pussies swimming. Some are hairy, some are smooth, some are big, and some are small.

A figure is standing over the edge and looking into the water. I stay down deep, holding my breath. It must be Peaches, the water warping my view of her wide figure. I'll stay down here until I black out, because there's no way I'm touching her again.

Seconds seem like hours. Time slows when you're underwater; the world is in a vacuum.

The figure leaves. Is she gone? My lungs are burning, so I erupt from the water and inhale air.

"Is she gone?" I ask, not seeing Peaches or Jazmin.

"Don't worry, sweetie. We got you covered," the busty blonde says.

"Why don't you stay awhile?" a brunette says. She goes under. I feel her at my feet. What is she doing? Then I feel her at my boxer shorts. I turn in circles, but I can't resist. She emerges with my shorts! The crowd cheers. I go to get them, but Jazmin comes out with her hands on her waist.

"I knew you were out here!" she yells.

I go to the edge and roll out of the water. I'm naked and I'm the attention of the entire pool!

Peaches clomps out. I go left, but Peaches cuts me off. I run right, but Jazmin blocks me. The brunette holds up my shorts and twirls them. The pool people holler.

There's a break between the two women, so I dash through the gap and explode into the house, while the audience outside starts clapping.

Those two fetching females are looking at me now. The one with the larger breasts eyes me and licks her lips. Her friend sucks on her finger. Oh man, I want to stay. Just five minutes.

"Get back here!" Peaches roars.

"Here comes two more to snack on," I say to the fetching females as I keep going.

Peaches and Jazmin don't take the bait.

The bartender comes around and sees me running. "Go, man, and I'll try to distract them," he says.

The eyes of the deer heads on the wall are staring at my naked body. Suddenly, there's a flicker in their eyes; it's Peaches stomping behind me. I divert into my room and grab my clothes, wallet, and cell phone, but Peaches makes it to the door.

"You're not getting away twice," she says.

Oh shit! What am I going to do?!

Jazmin arrives and stands at the door. Now, I'm really trapped. Peaches grabs my nearly empty Corona bottle. What is she going to do with it?

As I prepare to face my demise, a whistle in the hallway startles us. We all look out, seeing the bartender holding a plate with a sizzling steak, a side of steamed broccoli, and a perfectly cooked baked potato loaded with sour cream.

Peaches sniffs, her eyes wide. Then, she plows over Jazmin and thrusts through the door.

"Run!" the bartender yells.

Exploding out of the room, I dash toward the entryway. The toll keeper in the red dress looks at me with her eyes wide and white.

"Thanks again. I had fun," I say, smirking.

I push the door open and pour out of the house.

"Leaving so soon?" the doorman says.

"I'd stand back if I were you."

I make it to my car and hop inside, throwing my clothes on the passenger seat. I fire it up and slam it into reverse. The tires spin, kicking up stones, as Peaches charges from the doorway. I jam my car into drive and take off.

She hurls the Corona bottle toward me, smashing my passenger side mirror. "How dare you leave me!" she shouts.

Around a turn, the gate is in front of me. The gatekeeper runs to the control panel and presses a button. I'm going forty miles an hour toward the gate and I'm not stopping!

I hit it hard, causing the hood on my car to bend up.

The gate flies open as I turn, the tires squealing.

I've escaped! The mansion shrinks in my rear-view mirror until the purple flames extinguish. I look down at my penis as I drive away naked. What the hell am I doing? My mind hurts and the only thing I can do, the only thing I want to do, is to drive back to the lights.

# 12

How high is it? Eight hundred feet? No, it must be over a thousand. There's a green thing spinning on top. The screams of the people reach me all the way down here. If I had a girlfriend, I'd take her up there on top of the Stratosphere.

As my car idles at this traffic light, a cop on a motorcycle rolls up next to me. He's wearing black boots and his muscles are bulging out of his shirt. We lock eyes. I hold my breath as the dry air grazes my exposed skin. Is it against the law to drive with only a sock covering your penis?

"You know, it's illegal to operate a motor vehicle without a rear window," he says.

Oh, shit. I swallow hard. The red light burns my eyes. The screams from the top of the Stratosphere intensify.

The light turns green. I clutch the steering wheel. He's going to step on me with those boots. I'm going to jail. Geeks don't go to jail!

Suddenly, a pickup truck blows through the red light.

"At least put some clothes on," the cop says as he engages his red and blue lights and speeds after the pickup truck.

I have to get off the road and breathe some fresh air. I turn into the Stratosphere parking garage, find a secluded spot, and then get dressed. This car is going to get me killed.

Walking clears my mind. As I stroll down the Strip, the night is at its coolest, even though it's still seventy degrees out here. It's refreshing just to be free.

I walk past the Circus Circus. I would go in there if this were any other night.

Two lovely ladies are attached to a guy. They're coming my way, but they don't even look at me. Maybe I'm invisible. I need to go home, but Vegas already has me.

A red Ferrari is on display outside a casino with a seedy slot technician soliciting the walkers.

"Give her a pull! Win a car!" he says to a passing lady. "Come on, miss, try your luck."

He's chubby and wears a toupee. You can see it a mile away. He reminds me of George Costanza.

"There's a lonely face. Try your luck, kiddo," he says to me.

"Try my luck? What luck?" I reply, still walking.

"Luck changes on a dime in Vegas," he says.

The slot machine shows, "$1."

"You mean a dollar," I go.

"Go ahead and feed her a buck."

What do I have to lose, other than a dollar? I can lose that. After all, I've lost more than that tonight, and the night's not even over.

I engage the machine. Forget the button—I go for the lever. I want this to feel like a real pull, as if I have a chance to win with the right amount of strength and pressure.

The wheels spin. *Seven…Seven…Seven.* The machine buzzes. Lights flash.

"I won… I won! A new car! A Ferrari!"

"Well, kiddo, no car, but you just won five hundred bucks."

"What? No new car?" I say.

George Costanza radios on his walkie-talkie. "We have a five-hundred-dollar winner out here."

I can't believe I won something tonight. My muscles are tingling. It feels good. Hell, it feels great.

Two elderly women come over. They remind me of the old sisters who used to live next to my grandmother. Could this be them? But they died…unless Vegas is where lost souls travel.

"I've been gambling all night and didn't win a thing," the one with the gray hair says.

"I think this young stud should come with us," the other one says.

A sloppy slot technician with a beer gut comes out. "Who's the lucky winner?"

"This young stud," the gray-haired lady says.

The technician counts out five crisp one-hundred-dollar bills. They weigh a ton in my hand. I put them in my wallet.

"Now don't put it all back in," George Costanza says.

"Don't worry, I won't," I say, looking at the ladies.

"Who's the next lucky winner? Give her a pull! Win a car!" the guy continues.

I make a break for it. In and out with five hundred bucks in 90 seconds flat. Maybe tonight is my lucky night after all.

"Don't go!" the gray-haired lady yells.

"We could use your luck at all-night bingo," her friend says.

I don't look back. I wouldn't know what to do with those ladies, but they seem to know what to do with me.

After fifteen minutes of fresh air, I come up on the Treasure Island, which has a pirate ship out front. People are still admiring it, waiting for pirates, even though it's almost three a.m.

Street solicitors are cracking and popping cards in their hands. Are they handing out baseball cards? They're all over the ground. They look like baseball cards, but the players are all naked with stars covering their nipples. "$69 Special" is written across all of them. Oh, these are those girlie cards that I read about littering the streets of Sin City. These guys don't give up. There're probably a dozen of them hitting every passerby on both sides of the sidewalk. They even offer some old lady a card. What is she going to do with it?

The solicitor at the end of the group is wearing a bright neon T-shirt. He has a five o'clock a.m. shadow and a lean frame. Wait. Is that Javier? No… Yeah, that's Javier! He pops the cards in his hands and offers a few to a weary tourist. What the hell is Javier doing out here?!

I go up to him. "Club promoter, huh?"

He jumps at the sight of me. "Benjamin, my man, ya caught me," he says, still handing out the cards to the people like a trained monkey.

"I don't remember this class at Penn State."

"Hey, this is just a filler gig. Club promoting is during the day."

I shake my head. Everything is not as it seems in this town. "Hey, man, you gotta do what you gotta do," I reply.

He reaches around me to solicit a teenage boy.

"Hey, that's just a kid," I say.

"He's gotta learn sometime, right?" Javier says. "So, you scored?"

"Would I be wandering around the Strip if I scored?"

"It's not even three a.m. Come on, don't puss out," he says.

"I should ask if *you* scored. What happened to that Asian girl?"

"Oh, her," he says, smiling. "After our little rap video, I went back to her place. Well, let me tell ya. We went to her bedroom and I gave her one of my special—"

"Okay! You don't have to rub this in."

Javier doesn't dumb things down, sugarcoat them, or use tact to explain his knack. You must hear this story about him, but only if you're sitting down. One time at college on the morning after Halloween, I noticed water splashed all over the mirror and sink. I naturally confronted Javier. He started by telling me how he had been determined to bang an angel and a devil on Halloween. He found the devil at a party one of the basketball players was holding. Javier had no problem with her after a quarter bottle of vodka and a reservation in the back bedroom. He had trouble finding an angel, however. Nevertheless, he was not calling it a night until he shagged one. A half-hour before sunrise, he had to settle for a nun in a wheelchair. He said that he banged her so hard that the brakes disengaged, which sent her down a flight of stairs. He told me that a paralyzed woman could still get wet. In fact, he said that her vagina muscles clenched involuntarily, squeezing like an old man trying to get the last bit of toothpaste out. Then, he said that he came home and had to piss like a racehorse, but all that sex had his stream spraying at all angles. After that story, I skipped my morning class and bleached our bathroom.

"What about the black girl she was with? Did you find that place and bang her?" he asks.

"Uh, let's just say she had excess baggage, but I do have good news. I'm five hundred dollars richer, thanks to a slot machine."

Javier opens his eyes wide. Does he see someone?

"What?" I ask.

"Problem solved."

"What are you talking about?"

He flicks his cards. A guy with sunglasses and an Ohio State shirt grabs a handful. "Any man's problems can be solved for five hundred bucks in Vegas."

Javier retreats into the shadows. I watch the guy with the sunglasses. Javier does make sense. Five hundred is a lot of money, but the paid masseuse I had back in that West Hollywood massage parlor nearly broke my back.

Javier looks around and removes a card from his back pocket. He misses some people passing, but he doesn't miss me. He hands me the card.

"Oh, I don't know, man. I don't want to be one of *those* guys."

"Hey, it's Vegas," he says.

He's right. Five hundred bucks can solve not just any man's problems; it can solve *my* problems. It's house money. Just let the dice roll, right? I will set up the lady, go back, have my way with her, and then crash on the couch. At least, I'll be able to drift away into a deep sleep after the deed is done. Around eight a.m., I'll take a minute to call in to work, and then go back to sleep, waking up after eight hours, fully refreshed, my mojo flowing, my confidence back, my problems solved.

The card in my hand shows Vegas' finest pitcher. She has dark hair draped around her tanned skin. Her lips are bee-stung and complement her submissive eyes. Then there are her breasts. They are smaller than those on the other cards. They look natural, a handful for a football player, but I'm not a football player. I read the caption with a whisper, "Call Me – Diamond – $500 Special – An Hour You'll Never Forget."

"One of the independent girls left this," Javier says.

"A free agent, huh? Damn. She's…"

"I know. The independent ones don't mess around."

Her eyes are tempting. What color are they? I move the card in the light shining from the Treasure Island.

"Don't make love to it. You can have my place. Use the key I gave you. I'm working all night."

A man on a bike rides up with eyebrows permanently arched. He's wearing a black T-shirt, a deadly color out here on the road. "Keep them popping!"

The workers pick up the pace.

"I gotta get back to work. This guy used to be a tiger trainer for Siegfried & Roy."

"Thanks for looking out for me," I say, slapping Javier's hand.

"I got your back."

Although Javier and I fight like a married couple, we make up like kids. He's my ace in the pocket, my benefactor. No matter how I ridicule him or taunt him in my mind, he will always be my wingman.

A whip cracks. It's the guy on the bike whipping the street. Javier goes from being my old college roommate to a kitten succumbing to its master. If you think about it, he really is a cat.

I hide the card in my pocket and go to leave. The guy rolls down to the workers on the end of the sidewalk.

"Hey, Benjamin," Javier says.

I turn.

"For the next hour…you're Javier."

"Let's move it, *muchacho*!" the man on the bike yells.

"Hey, lay off! I'm helping my friend get laid," Javier shouts.

Geez, don't announce it to the whole street! The guy on the bike slaps the sidewalk in front of Javier, who starts passing out cards furiously. I'd better get out of here.

The walk back to the Stratosphere takes forever. I hope my car is still there. That's all I need is to have it stolen. That poor car, it's not even paid off!

I'm jogging with the tower in my view, but I can't hold it any longer. I stop to call the number on the card.

Dialing is hard as I keep looking into her eyes. They're telling me to call, to let her keep her eyes on me for an hour. It's ringing. What if she's not home? She probably has a client. A girl this stunning must have clients lined up outside her door. I start biting my lip. Ahh, what am I doing? This is stupid. But just as my finger rests on the "end" button, the phone clicks.

"Hello?" she says, her voice deep, not in a manly sense, but in a fuck-me-all-night sense.

What was Javier saying? I take a deep breath. I'm going to go back to his place, going to use his stuff, going to get laid on his bed. For the next hour, I'm going to roll like him. I'm going to be Javier.

"Uh, is this…" I start to say in my best Latino accent.

"…Diamond?" she finishes.

"*Sí*… I mean, yeah."

"It is, sweetie. Who is this?" she goes.

"My name is Javier."

"Latino, huh? How did you get my number?"

"That's not important. What is important is I would like to purchase your one-hour special."

"I like a guy who knows what he wants. I'm available now."

I glance at my watch and see that it's five after three. "Let's make it three thirty. And the fee is five hundred?"

"Yeah, five hundred, but I do have some important ground rules."

"Oh, I don't need to use the, uh, you know, *backdoor*," I reply.

"Sweetie, these rules are much more important than sticking your dick in my butt."

Oh, no, here we go. A woman's ground rules are rules that can never be broken, or she will put you into the ground. One time, I heard a woman say to Javier at a party that she had ground rules. I never heard what they were exactly, but Javier came home later with a black eye. He never did tell me that story, but this is Vegas where the ground is so dry, it can't be penetrated.

"Okay, I'm listening," I reply.

"Do you live in a gated community?"

"No. Why is that important?"

"That's for me to decide. And you must be alone. It's very, very important."

"Don't worry, honey. It'll be just me, Benjamin Franklin, and his four cloned brothers."

"I like your speed. Can you text me the address?"

"You got it."

"See you at three thirty, tiger. I'll make you a new man."

I text the address to her, and the deal is done. This is it. It's all falling into place. The five-hundred-dollar win was a sign to buy what I lacked, but was it a sign from above or from below?

My car is still at the Stratosphere. It's smashed, dented, scratched, but strangely, it doesn't bother me. Perhaps it's because I'm too tired; perhaps it's something else.

As I start to drive to Javier's place, my father is on my mind. He always goes to church every Saturday at 5:00. I used to go with him. I liked going to church, but ever since moving out West, I haven't sat in any pews. What does God think about me now? What is my place supposed to be on this planet? It's so hard to find my way sometimes. Look at me tonight. I'm stooping down to pay for sex. Is this legal? Moral? I don't really know. Why I'm thinking about this here and now, I don't really know either. Nevertheless, I do know that the East and the West Coasts are two gravely different places. The

West Coast has changed me. I used to detest haggling with a car salesman back East, being afraid of hurting his feelings, but now out West, I bizarrely crave it. I have those people I deal with on a daily basis, my coworkers and the acquaintances I chat with, like the older lady who parks next to me in the parking garage or the waitress at Panera Bread, Emily or Emmy. I have my people and that's it. Everyone else, everyone not in my circle, like the car salesman, forces me to play a game. I can be that rude kid who haggles over the price. Back East, you try to make everyone your friend. In the West, you try *not* to make everyone your friend.

# 13

A traffic light turns red. There's a billboard in front of me showing Penn & Teller sawing each other, their heads and the saw extending beyond the top of the billboard. When did billboards stop being rectangular? What's next, spinning objects and bright lights to get your attention? And they wonder why there're so many accidents!

Diamond's card is in my hand. Her eyes are telling me to relax, to let her remove all of my worries. She's right.

In the parking lot for Javier's apartment, all the cars are asleep. It's 3:16 on my clock, plenty of time to get ready.

I trudge up the steps and use the key. The apartment is dark. Where is the light switch? I bump into an end table, searching the wall. Something is gooey. Yuck! Finally, I flick what I think is the switch; the lights come on. I shut the front door and look at the bottles of booze on the cheetah-patterned rug. Were there empty bottles there when I left? Hmm…

I go to the back bedroom and find the light switch. Dirty clothes litter the room. Sheets are strewn across the full-size bed. The room stinks of sweat. I'm not going in there!

I shut off the lights and move back toward the living room. What's inside that other room? Grace Kelly knows, but she won't tell me.

The couch is the best place to do the deed. It's leather and I've never been laid on leather. I push the coffee table away to provide more room. How tall is Diamond? It would be awesome if she is taller than I am.

I grab the bottles, but one with some beer left falls onto the couch. Shit. I wipe it up with a kitchen towel and flip the cushion over—good as new.

Letting out a sigh, I take a seat. This will be the spot that I become a real man, the spot that will take me to places I've never been before. I'm not nervous, not anxious. I'm excited that it's going to happen. It's so much easier this way. Money really does talk.

Javier's robe is hanging over a kitchen chair. The clock on the wall shows, "3:25."

What are these ground rules that Diamond has? Why does it matter whether I live in a gated community? Does she not know how to drive through a gate? There's really no logic to this, or to this whole city for that matter.

My stomach growls. That hamburger in Barstow was my last meal. Is it okay to have sex on an empty stomach? There're only four minutes left. Oh, shit. This is happening soon. I take a deep breath as my stomach growls again.

I sprint to the fridge. Inside are bottles of Corona on every shelf and inside every drawer. One is even resting on top of the tray with the cutouts for eggs. There're more bottles in this fridge than in the fridge inside the office of Corona's CEO. The only thing visible that's not a bottle is on the top shelf, a shot glass with something swimming around inside it. As I spin the glass around, the label hits me: "In-Home Sperm Testing Kit." I slam the door shut! Yuck!

In the freezer, the place where no fornicating fungi can live, there are frozen pizzas and Hot Pockets. The sight reminds me of college. There's a box of SuperPretzels. My favorite! These only take 35 seconds to cook. In goes one into the microwave.

All I need now is mustard, but I'm not looking back in that refrigerator. I open some drawers and see some sandwich bags and twist ties. Another drawer has knives—this one might come in handy. Then, buried under paper plates are some mustard packets, the spicy kind. Spicy sounds good. I open one, missing the "Tear here" on the other side of the packet. Why do they have to print that? People know that tearing is the only way inside. I can see if there really is only one spot to tear, but there's not. You can tear this thing on any side. They should just print instructions that say, "Tear anywhere."

My belly is now full. Javier's robe on that chair calls me. Hmm. He did say to be Javier.

It's now 3:30 on the button. I'm standing in front of the mirror wearing Javier's robe, gumming the pipe—I cleaned it, of course. So this is how the master likes to play. This getup does make me stand tall and sport a grin. I should walk around like this in my home. Maybe this is what I needed all along.

A knock sounds at the door, causing me to drop the pipe from my mouth. The weight of a thousand bricks hits me inside the room. Can I really go through with this? What if she laughs at me? I can't take that type of rejection. I shouldn't be wearing this robe. I shouldn't be here. Maybe I shouldn't answer it, but the card on the table is glistening. Diamond is waiting.

I open the door as if I'm removing a Band-Aid. Diamond has come alive. Chopsticks hold up her hair. Her lips are moist, and her eyes suck me in. Wow, this is for me! This is all for me! My knees weaken.

"Well, hello there," I say.

"What happened to the accent?" she chuckles.

I clear my throat and try to correct it. "I mean, *hello there*."

"You look like Bill Gates trying to impersonate Hugh Hefner."

"I'm a mix between a man and amazing."

She shakes her head and smirks. "You said your name was…"

"*Javier*."

"Ha! Well, I'll call you whatever you want."

"Please come in," I say, offering her the house and losing the accent.

She steps inside, holding a small purse. She's wearing a black dress that starts low and ends high. Her breasts look round, not too big, not too small. They jiggle when she walks. Blood rushes to my groin.

Her expression is all business as she scans the apartment like a home inspector looking for faulty workmanship. "Are you alone?" she asks.

"Yes, don't worry."

What's her problem? Does she think I have my little brother hiding in the closet?

"No roommates or vicious dogs?" she continues.

"What are you so concerned about?" I ask.

"Hey, I told you I have very specific rules."

"Ground rules, right?"

"Exactly, but you seem harmless enough."

"Is that a good thing?" I ask.

She chuckles…again. A little crease forms between her eyes when she laughs. What does that mean? Is it a crease of deception or a crease of seduction? She should be in a business suit, walking behind the tellers at the bank, ogling the money with those sexy eyes. She doesn't set her bag down. She walks while looking at everything but me. Is she a cop? Maybe she is. No, she can't be a cop. Javier vouched for her. Stop thinking!

"Business first," she goes.

She really is a businesswoman. I can respect that. What's under that dress, Diamond? Please show me. I walk over to my pants and remove my wallet, grabbing the five Benjamins.

"Five hundred, right?" I say.

"Thank you, sweetie," she replies, taking the money. "Now, I have only one more rule."

My scalp itches. "Please, no more rules," I say.

"Well, I have to give this to my driver. He's waiting for me and if I don't come out within five minutes, he's instructed to come in with a gun."

Oh my God! Another gun! What the hell is going on? I look outside at the moon. Is SWAT going to storm the place?

This whole thing is making the spicy mustard come back up my throat. Did the hour already start?

"Driver? I don't like this," I say.

"Sweetie, it's just how this type of business is conducted out here. Think of it from *my* perspective."

She does have a point, but you'd think Javier would've said something to me. Why would he miss this glaring detail? I never remember him worrying about a driver with a gun back at Penn State.

She comes close and fondles my robe with her hand. Her scent sends a thousand pins into my scalp. She wouldn't wear this perfume if she didn't want to have sex. "Once I take care of this, then I can take care of you," she goes. Now she's looking at me. "Go get me a drink."

"Of water?" I ask.

"Only if you freeze that water and surround it with gin and tonic."

"Gin and tonic, hmm." My eyes go to the time bomb called the fridge.

"Actually, whatever you're having is fine. I'll be right back." Diamond steps out, leaving me alone.

She's right. This is a dangerous city and a girl needs protection. It makes total sense. I'm going to have a Corona. Do you think she likes Corona? She does come off as more of a gin and tonic kind of girl, but she said for me to get her whatever I'm having, and I'm having a Corona.

Holding my breath, I swing open the door to the refrigerator. On the bottom shelf, I grab two bottles, and then slam the door shut. A little blue shark with the words *Key Largo, FL* is stuck to the side of the fridge. He still has it! That thing was stuck to the side of our fridge in our college dorm in Happy

Valley. It probably has opened thousands of beer bottles, some for me, most for him. I open both Coronas and sit down on the couch.

Those were the days at Happy Valley. Is there a way to go back? Life was so much simpler back then with clear objectives: pass your test, call home, wash your clothes. Now, I'm worried about car payments and doing presentations for people double my age. In college, everyone is around your age. It bonds you together, gives you the ability to sit next to your friends, and to stand as one. The hardest decade in your life is your twenties. You're beyond the babysitter years in high school. Face it, you can't really do anything without your parents' approval in high school. When you turn twenty, you have broken free from the apron strings. You go to bed when you want, eat what you want, and befriend who you want.

Then college ends, and you're thrown into something called the workforce, where you're forced to find a way to survive. You're not supposed to settle down; that comes when you're in your thirties. My uncle kept saying for me to spread my wings, live a little, explore. But what if you don't have wings?

There were so many pathways when I had graduated at 22. Should I go back home now to the Poconos in Pennsylvania? But there are no technical jobs there, just blue-collar labor. My cousins are making bottle caps and molding chocolate for Hershey. I can't do that. I *won't* do that.

Moving was my only real option. I thought moving to the West was the path for me, since my mom was always commenting on the CGI in movies when I was growing up. I remember seeing *Titanic* with her in high school, and she said that I could do all that computer imagery. I thought it would be so cool to do that type of work, but here I am, three years later after college, in a dead-end job with a horrible boss. I can't find a girlfriend. Hell, I can't even find a friend. Here I am at three in the morning, sitting in someone else's shitty apartment, wearing his clothes, with a bottle of beer in my hand, waiting for a hooker to give my five-hundred dollars to her driver, so he doesn't shoot me. Will I even make it out of my twenties?

It's now 3:35. Diamond has been out there for too long. What the hell is she doing? What the hell am I doing? I should just go home, my real home in PA. I should just keep driving. How long is it from NV to PA?

I'm going to get dressed. My pants are by the TV, so I grab them and put them on while still wearing the robe. My cell phone is in my pocket, but where's my wallet? Oh yeah, it's on the table. But it's not there. Wait! It was just there!

"Diamond!" I yell.

I run out of the apartment and look over the banister. An SUV is squealing around a turn. That's her!

"That bitch!" I yell.

People are giggling nearby. A man and a woman are entering their apartment, laughing at me.

I go back inside. Shit! The money is one thing, but that wallet has my driver's license, my credit cards, my work I.D.! I can just hear Ms. Dipple saying, "Lose your badge, your job loses you."

I'm dead.

What am I going to do? If I call the cops, do I tell them that a hooker robbed me? This whole thing looks bad. Should I call Javier? What's he going to do? Damn it, I need to do something right now. Should I see if I can find that SUV? What should I do?

I throw a kitchen chair across the room in anger. There's her card. I tear it in half.

The front door explodes open. Who is this guy? A cop? The driver? He's wearing a sparkling gold shirt and black slacks. Wait, is this the guy from when I first came here? Yeah, he's the burly guy who passed me in the hall. What the hell is he doing here?

"Who the hell are you?" I say.

"No, who the hell are *you*? And what're you doing in my place?"

"Your place?" I say.

"Yeah. My place."

"This is Javier's apartment."

"This is *my* apartment. Javier rents that shabby room back there." He looks at me with mean eyes. "What are you doing in his robe?"

"Long story. I'm Benjamin, his old college roommate."

"Oh, so you're the computer geek." He takes his eyes off me and walks toward Grace Kelly, unlocking the door. "Well, keep it down, because I'm going to bed."

The guy seals himself behind Grace. My cell phone rings. I'm more popular at 3:30 in the morning than at 3:30 in the afternoon. The screen reads, "Unknown."

"Hello?" I say.

"Benny, boy. What are we going to do with you?" a female voice says.

Is that Jazmin, or is it Ms. Dipple? No, it can't be. The voice has an accent, a Russian accent. Wait. I know who it is. "Uh, is this…"

"Yeah, it is. You have my matchbook."

"Matchbook? What are you talking about?"

"The matchbook you took from my room."

"Natasha, how did you get this number?"

"That's what I do, Benjamin. And you're becoming the thorn in my side on this mission."

That matchbook was the parting gift from the game show I lost. It's gone, right along with my life. "Well, I don't have the matchbook anymore, because it was stolen by a hooker."

"A hooker?! That matchbook has codes for my targets."

"Well, it's in my wallet that she took, which also has my work I.D. badge."

"Who gives a shit about your work I.D. badge? I need that matchbook!" she yells through the phone.

"What can I say?"

"What happened?" she asks.

"I called the number that was on her business card. I was supposed to get one hour with her for five hundred bucks, and well, she scammed me."

"Benjamin, you need to get laid."

"I'm accepting applications."

"Do you have her phone number?" she asks.

I grab both pieces of Diamond and line up her torso to her legs.

"Yeah, I have it. Five Five Four One Nine Eight One."

"Okay, I'll get her address. You stay put."

"Hey! No way! She has my I.D. badge."

"Ugh..." she exhales. "Okay, just let me handle all the dirty work. I'll call you back."

“Now we’re talking!” I say.

She hangs up. I remove the robe and put on the rest of my clothes, the clothes that I came here with, but I leave off the tie. A real spy is going to help me get my I.D. back, and not just any spy, but a sexy Russian spy. This is awesome! I feel good. No, I feel fucking great.

I’m sprinting to my car when I see a windowless van in the parking lot marked, “Happy Florist.” As I approach my car, there’s a husky dude with a shaved head holding flowers and walking to the van. He goes in the rear door and for a split second, a glimmer of light reflects off the tanned skin of a woman inside the van. The image is so familiar. Is that… No, it can’t be.

My phone rings again.

“Hello?”

“Okay, I got her address,” Natasha says.

Something fishy is going on here. I walk toward the windowless van. “That’s not surprising,” I reply.

“How well do you know Vegas?” she goes.

“I should ask *you* that question.”

“What’s wrong with you?”

“What kind of flowers do you like?” I ask, ten feet from the van.

“What are you talking about?”

The van is spotless, a pristine product from the production line. The overhead lights glow in the white paint. What florist keeps a van this spotless? The sign for “Happy Florist” is a magnet. I knock on the van, and then I hear the same knock delayed a few seconds inside the phone.

“I know you’re in there!” I shout, my heart pounding.

Suddenly, the side door slides open and Natasha jumps out. Before she closes the door, I catch two guys checking surveillance cameras and adjusting headsets. Natasha grabs my hand and pulls me to the side of the building. Her hand is so warm, so soft.

"You're going to blow my cover," she shouts inside a whisper, still clutching my hand.

"Are you following me?" I ask.

"No, I'm following your friend."

"Javier?"

"Why are you always complicating things?" she goes.

"Tell me why the Russians are after my college roommate."

"He's been hacking into the computers in our embassy."

"Javier? Hacking? I think you've got the wrong guy. Javier only knows how to look up porn on his computer."

"Listen, a virus was created on his computer and was used to infect our servers. The virus is stealing secrets."

"Javier is stealing Russian secrets? Come on. Am I dreaming? I must be, because beautiful women never hold my hand."

She flings my hand away with a fire still burning in her eyes. "We know it's his computer. We have his IP address, along with two other computers infected with this virus."

"On the matchbook. I knew I recognized one of those numbers, but why did you write them on a matchbook? Don't you have copies?"

"It's a long story. We're just figuring some of this out now. We sifted through thousands of IP addresses and—why am I telling you this?" she says.

"By only writing them on a matchbook, you messed up, didn't you? Ha, I know the feeling. One time—"

"Listen, *you* messed this up."

"But wait, Javier is not a computer hacker. You've got the wrong guy."

"Hey, we're all somebody different out here. You should know that," she says, raising her eyebrows.

Could Javier really be that smart? Could he really be a hacker? Why did he call me out here and play dumb? Maybe he's trying to frame me. No. This isn't Javier. I shared two years with him at Penn State. He was either drunk or hung over. I did all his work for the only computer class he took. Something is weird about this. Who is this woman?

"What are you going to do?" I ask her.

"Well, we're going to get that matchbook back. That's what we're going to do."

"Javier is innocent. I know it. If I can—"

"We'll worry about that later, but for now, I need that matchbook. Those guys in that van don't speak English, so if you want to explain to them how you lost it, then be my guest."

"Where are we going?" I ask.

"I'll text you the address."

"Can't I just follow you?"

"I'm not your mother. I'll meet you there. I have to go talk to my colleagues and convince them that you are required to accomplish this mission."

"What if they don't buy it?"

"They will handcuff you, gag you, and put a bag over your head. Then they will interrogate you. They are from the old Soviet days."

"But I don't speak Russian."

"You will by the time they're done with you. Now go," she says.

"Sounds like a plan. Hey, I love this James Bond stuff."

"Benjamin, don't pull any more of your stunts! I mean it! Just stay in your car when you get there and wait for my instructions."

"Roger that," I reply.

I head back to my car, not making eye contact with the Happy Florists. Flowers are nice, but not flowers that only grow in Russia. My car is dented, dinged, smashed, slashed, and partially demolished, but it still fires up.

My phone rings. Again, the caller ID says, "Unknown." Is everyone anonymous in this town?

"People are going to think we're dating with all these calls," I say, pulling out of the parking lot.

"Hey, asshole! Did you have fun?" an angry male shouts into my ear.

"Who the hell is this?" I reply.

"The husband of the woman you screwed."

I furrow my brow. "I think you've got the wrong guy."

"Cut the shit! Jazmin. I saw your text messages on her phone."

"Dude, I didn't screw your wife. I gotta go." I press the button to end the call. There's no time for games now.

I turn toward the Stratosphere. That thing is a great focal point. My phone beeps. It's a new text message with the location where my life awaits.

# 14

My lips are dry. Maybe there's some lip balm in the glove box. The air out here is so dry. I didn't notice it when I first got here, but now my skin is cracking.

I'm driving down Mountain Cliff Drive. That's what it says in the text. I found it by calling information on my phone. Why didn't I think to do that before? I have to start thinking like a spy.

This street reminds me of Santa Monica. There are grass yards and a lot of trees. How did they get trees in the desert? Did they plant them or ship them?

The text says, "7306." Dormant homes surround me. One of the house numbers reads, "7304." The house next to it is the one I want. It's dark inside. I should keep going. I can't park out front. That's probably rule number one in spy school.

There's an open spot in front of a house with its lights on. It's shabby with boards on one window and desert gravel instead of grass. The house is talc among diamonds.

I turn off the headlights and the engine. The sound of heavy bass music spews from the shabby house as the shadows of bodies dance in the windows. Wow, people really do party all night here.

In the rear-view mirror, darkness fills the street. My finger jackhammers the steering wheel. Where is she? It's 4:19 on the clock in my car. She told me to wait for her, so I'll wait. I lick my lips again. Oh yeah, the lip balm.

I open my glove box and find a flashlight. All spies need a flashlight, right? See, I'm already prepared. I turn it on, but it's dead. Hitting it in my hand only gives me a trickle of light for a second. In the compartment of the flashlight are two AA batteries. Do I have new batteries?

In the glove box, there're some napkins, some electrical tape, and my insurance papers. Buried at the bottom is a copper top. A battery! It's a C. Shit! That won't work, so I toss the dead flashlight back inside. They should do away with batteries. It's the year 2007 and they still have battery technology from the Cold War era. Why do they have AA and AAA? Is there an A battery? And why aren't there any B batteries? What happened to those? They go right to C and D. What's wrong with this world?!

I step into the darkness and take a deep breath. The coolness in the air slows my breathing. As I push the car door closed, it only clicks once. Shit! I have to push harder to get it all the way shut. Why are there two clicks?! The idiot who designed car doors with two levels of closed should be shot!

I flee the car and look at the shabby house. I'm tiptoeing down the sidewalk when I see two male partiers peering through the window with a cloud of smoke around them. Wait. That double chin and those pearly whites look so familiar. Is that… Yeah! That's Smokin' and that chubby guy. Oh shit! I keep going. Did they see me? No. It's too dark out here.

Now, I'm right out front of 7306, which is Diamond's house. There's a waist-high fence, but that shouldn't be a problem.

A car approaches with headlights like spotlights in a prison yard.

"Oh shit," I mutter, ducking behind a parked car as the vehicle passes.

It's dark again. Should I hop over the fence by swinging my legs to the left or to the right? Or should I just step over it? Stop overthinking this!

I trot toward the fence and jump, but clip my left shoe on the top. I spill onto the ground. Did anyone see me? This is embarrassing. At least this grass softened my fall. How does grass grow in the desert anyway?

The place is two stories tall with dark stucco siding. As I move closer to the door, a dog bone is on the ground, as well as a dish the size of a horse trough. Around the side of a tree is a doghouse. Oh, no, not another dog. What do I do?

I creep across the grass. Maybe it's asleep.

*Squeak*! I step on a spongy ball.

Something moves inside the doghouse. My heart starts pounding. This could be bad.

A little poodle scurries out, tail wagging, tongue dangling. It doesn't bark, but what dog doesn't bark?

"Nice doggy," I say as it watches me.

Something else moves inside the doghouse. Is it another poodle?

A monster comes out. It looks like a Doberman, and it's eyeing its next meal, but maybe it likes computer geeks.

As I take a small step toward the door, the big dog growls and shows me its teeth.

"There's a good boy."

It comes toward me and buries its snout into my crotch. I need to get laid, but this is not how I want to do it. The dog is sniffing my pocket. What is it doing? There's something in there that it wants. Inside is the candy that Ms. Dipple gave me.

"Here, want some candy?" I drop it in the yard.

The dog takes the bait. I'm free! I go back the way I came and hop over the fence. This time, I make it over without falling. What's that scent in the air? It's sweeter than the freshest huckleberry pie my grandmother used to make. I step backward into a shadowy figure.

"I told you to stay in your car," Natasha says.

"I know, but I couldn't help it."

"What did you find over there?"

"It looks like she has some dogs, but the big one's a sucker for candy."

"Rule number one is that you never go through the front door without a plan. Do you see her car?" she says.

Sedans and coupes line the street. "No, I think she has an SUV, but I didn't really get a good look."

"Well, just stay close. Maybe the matchbook is inside."

Following her lead, I stay on her tail. She's still wearing that same killer black dress. Her hair blows back when she moves, brushing against my face, her sweet aroma melting my mind.

We go to the side of the house.

"I'll help you over the fence," I say.

Natasha opens the gate with one finger. I shrug. Before we move forward, the ring on her right ring finger flashes. She presses her left finger into her ear and speaks into the ring. What the hell is she doing?

"*Da*," she says, listening. Then she looks at me. "*Da. Da*." Her eyes hit the ground and she bites her lip. "*Da*." She lowers her hands.

"Are they mad?" I ask, but she ignores me and continues through the shadows around the house.

"So we are like both spies now," I say, trying to keep up.

"Don't flatter yourself."

"Listen, I was thinking about all this. You really do have the wrong guy. I mean, Javier might be known for stealing a few beers from the neighbor's fridge, but stealing Russian secrets?"

She stops and looks at me, her eyes narrowing. "I believe you, but those guys in the van, those *angry Russians*, they don't believe you; they only believe what's in that matchbook, so let's get it, and then get the hell out of here, okay?"

"Roger that."

She'd better be telling the truth. Is this whole thing going to work out? Why did I come to this damn town again?

Little cacti are lining the walkway. Cacti are cool. One on my desk would be nice.

As we make it to the side of the house, she checks the door, and finds that it's locked. I stand back, awaiting the professional to make her next move. She goes over to a breaker box on the wall; it's locked too.

The streetlights are reflecting off her legs. Wow! They look good, damn good. How would it be to rub my hands on them and follow them up under her dress? However, as I stand here dreaming, Natasha reaches between her legs, acting out my fantasy. Oh my! What's she doing? She pulls out a small screwdriver from under her dress and opens the breaker box.

"What else do you have up there?" I whisper.

She winks at me.

A plethora of wires is inside the box. She hands me the screwdriver. I want to sniff it, but that's just weird. Maybe if she weren't looking.

"What are you doing?" I ask.

"Checking for a security system."

"I bet this doubles as a detonation device," I say, looking at the screwdriver. There are Cyrillic letters written on its metal.

"Are you serious?" she goes.

"Which wire do we cut? The blue or the red."

She looks at me and shakes her head. "Okay. Doesn't look like any security system."

Natasha puts the cover back on and snatches the screwdriver from me. She moves to the door and fishes under her dress again, this time removing a small pouch. Are they condoms? No. Inside the pouch are some little metal tools. What is she doing? She puts a tool into the lock and starts to tinker with it.

"Cool!" I say.

"Shh..."

"So how long have you been doing this spy stuff?"

"This is my first assignment," she says.

"Damn, really?"

"And I don't want it to be my last. You already messed things up for me."

She has a twinge in her voice, which causes my breathing to stop. Who is Natasha? Sure, she's sexy, provocative, blunt, strong, enigmatic, but who is the *real* Natasha? Does she have an old college roommate too? I exhale and say, "Hey, I'm sorry about all this."

As she grips the handle and twists the tool in the lock, the door opens. "Save your sorry for someone else."

Natasha goes under her dress again. I'm afraid to look, but all she pulls out is a small flashlight.

"I was going to bring mine, but I didn't have any batteries. I know a flashlight is standard issue for spies."

As I babble, Natasha has already entered the house. I go to the door, but it's pitch black inside. "Natasha, are you there?"

She emerges from the shadows and pulls me inside as I close the door behind me. Now we're standing inside the living room. My eyes try to adjust, allowing the filtered streetlights to guide me. Natasha uses the flashlight to check the living room. In the middle is a couch. An LCD television graces the wall. A stripper pole stands in the corner. Have I been here before?

"This reminds me of the one time at college when Javier was drunk and—"

"Shh, you talk too much."

She shines the light into the attached kitchen and onto the refrigerator.

"Doesn't look like anyone's home," I say.

"Great work, Mr. Bond. Let's check the bedrooms."

She doesn't waste any time. She moves like the shadows. I follow her down the hallway and into a bedroom. Natasha shines the light around the dresser. Makeup containers are everywhere. The scent of apples is in the air. This has to be Diamond's room. There's a bookcase in the corner. Is that leather? Wait. Is that my wallet?

"Over there. Shine some light," I say.

She shines the light and I go to investigate. What I thought was a wallet is actually a Coach handbag, but then I see something on the top shelf. "Whoa!"

"What did you find?" she asks.

"She has all the seasons of *Seinfeld* on DVD."

She slaps the back of my head. "Straighten up."

Natasha sits on the bed.

"What are you doing?" I ask.

"Well, now we must wait."

"A stakeout, huh?" I say.

"Waiting is the number one duty with this job. Just be quiet. I need to think."

I sit down next to her. A clock is ticking from somewhere in the shadows, hypnotically, rhythmically. I can feel my heart beating inside my chest. It's beating faster than the clock, but I take a deep breath and try to slow it down, try to marry it to the clock.

What time is it on the clock, anyway? It has to be nearly five a.m. Is Natasha listening to the clock too? Although she didn't give me my first taste of a real Vegas encounter, she did give me many firsts tonight. She talked to me in code, kissed me to hide her cover, held a pistol on me, and shared some of her tradecraft. What does she think about me?

"Natasha. I just want to say again that I'm sorry for—"

"Shh…" she goes.

I hold my tongue. I'm not doing myself a service here.

Then after thirty more beats of the clock, Natasha says, "What's the first thing you would do if you found out that you were going to die?"

"I don't know. Stop brushing my teeth."

"I'm serious, Benjamin."

"I'm sorry. That's a tough question. I'm not really sure. Are you dying or something?"

She doesn't respond right away, which twists my stomach.

"Well, I'm not dying, but my *babushka*…grandmother in Russian…was just diagnosed with colon cancer. The doctors gave her three months left to live."

As my stomach twists even tighter, I lick my lips. They're still dry, but I've accepted it. "I'm so sorry."

"Thank you," she says.

"I only have one of my grandmothers left, my mom's mom. She lives in Pennsylvania."

"How often do you see her?"

"Not often enough."

"You should, because I regret not seeing my *babushka*. I've been working for the Russian government for over a year now."

"It must be such a cool job."

"It's not like the movies. They give you all this training, and then more training, but the assignments are mostly babysitting jobs." She shines the light on me. "But, you know, I worked so hard in college, sacrificed so much to get top grades. I always wanted to work for the Russian government.

Now that it's happened, I feel…empty. I miss my family. I've learned that family is the most important thing to me."

The knot in my stomach unravels. "You sound just like me. My biggest thing is that the people I work with are so old. It makes me feel…"

"…old," she finishes.

We chuckle. "How old are you, if you don't mind me asking?" I say.

"Twenty-six."

"Ha! So am I," I say. "You know, this crazy night aside, I totally understand how you feel. After college, I moved across America, three thousand miles away from home. I thought what I wanted is out here in the West, but I haven't found it yet and I'm swirling down the drain. I don't think I'll find what I want out here. I'm all alone."

"I'm all alone too."

Then, my heart rate breaks free from the clock. It's too dark to see, but I turn my head on instinct and move forward through the darkness, and what I feel does more than excite me. It makes me feel wanted, makes me feel *not alone*. Natasha's lips touch mine as we kiss. I caress her body, feel her warmth, sense her soul. Her arms embrace me and let me know that she too is in this moment with me. As she holds me, and as I hold her, for this moment in time, a moment that will last only a few ticks of the clock, yet will last forever, I fall truly and deeply in love with her.

The sound of the front door opening stops us. We break our embrace. There's always someone walking in when I open my heart. Light from the living room spills into the bedroom.

"You're okay, Benjamin," she whispers with a soft voice that will forever stay with me.

How should I reply? But she's already standing, so I go back to following her.

"Should we confront her?" I whisper.

"No, not yet. We don't know for sure it's her, so let's just watch and wait." She scurries into the closet.

"Hey, let me in," I say.

"There's only enough room for one. You say you want to be a spy. Go find somewhere else to hide," she says, shutting the door.

Should I hide under the bed? No, I don't think I'd fit. There's only the attached bathroom, so I go inside. More women's stuff is in here than in the women's aisle at the 99-cent store: hair spray, toothpaste, shaving lotion, tubes of lipstick, tubes of ChapStick, mascara, blush, dental floss, Listerine, Scope, contact lens solution, eye drops, hand lotion, sunscreen, spray deodorant, roll-on deodorant, and cold cream. There's only one place I can hide, the bathtub, so I get in, pull the curtain closed, and wait.

From this angle, the moon is visible through the window above me. Back in my apartment, the moon is visible when I lie in my bed. I look at it sometimes at night to pacify me after a boring day alone, and while I am far, far away from my bed, the moon still pacifies me.

The bedroom lights illuminate. I widen my eyes. Is Natasha going to jump her? But her words of wisdom said to wait.

The bathroom lights come on. I hold my breath. This is it. Natasha had better save me. But what if she's no longer there?

The toilet seat goes up. Then there is silence. Is she peeing? What's going on? I can't handle this. I hear the sound of whistling. I know the feeling, Diamond.

Three loud bangs erupt from the front door.

"Who the hell is this?" Diamond says.

She flushes the toilet, and then the lights go out. Who could be banging? Those bangs sounded aggressive. Who bangs like that at five in the morning? I'm afraid to find out, but I'm even more afraid to find out lying in a bathtub.

I go back into the bedroom and whisper, "Natasha. Hey, Natasha."

I open the closet and see a pistol pointing at my face. "Whoa!"

"Shh, what are you doing?" she says.

"Let's make our move. It's her."

"Where is he?" a male voice roars from the living room.

Natasha looks at me. "Is he looking for you?"

I shrug. How could this guy be looking for me?

Natasha goes to the door and peers down the hall. Should I go? Natasha should handle this, but she waves me over.

"What?" Diamond says from down the hall.

I look over Natasha's shoulder. The guy is wearing thick glasses and a white shirt and tie. He looks familiar; he looks like me. Rage consumes his face, present in the divot between his eyes.

"Where's the guy who slept with my wife?" he goes.

"Are you on drugs?" Diamond says. Her breasts jiggle from her forceful reply. Wow, she's damn fine for a con artist. You know what would be hot? She should take one of those chopsticks from her hair and stab him. Then, she and Natasha could fight it out with their claws. Now that would be some show.

The guy raises a PDA-looking device in his hand. “The man who slept with my wife is in this house.”

“That’s impossible!” Diamond says.

“This thing says his cell phone is somewhere in this house,” the guy continues.

I lean forward into Natasha’s hair. Ahh, that aroma returns. “Is that really a cell phone tracker?” I ask.

Natasha looks at me, her eyes saying to shut up.

“I don’t know what’s going on, but you’ve got the wrong place,” Diamond says.

“Well, who the hell are you?” he says to Diamond. He’s looking at the stripper pole. “Is that all that’s in this town? Whores and con artists?”

“Listen, asshole! You can take that device and shove it up your ass! Get outta my house!”

“How far are we going to let this go?” I whisper to Natasha. She raises her left pointer finger and grips the pistol with her right hand.

The guy muscles past Diamond. “I know you’re hiding him!”

“There’s no one here but me!” she yells.

Natasha slides out and raises her cool pistol. “That’s not quite true.”

“And who the hell are you?” Diamond shouts.

“It appears you have something of mine,” Natasha says.

She talks so sexily. Is *sexily* even a word? Her voice is nonchalant, yet commanding. She has the power to woo a man with her words and to taunt a woman with her tone.

Diamond looks around her living room. "Okay, am I being punk'd? Where's the camera?"

"Tell her, Benjamin," Natasha says.

Watching this is enjoyable, but now I must enter the lion's den. I walk out with a culpable smile.

"You!" Diamond says, widening her eyes.

"Thought you could scam me, huh? Well, you messed with the wrong guy," I say, standing behind my Russian temptress.

"How did you find me?" Diamond says, her eyes narrowing.

"Ha-ha! That's what spies do," I reply.

Jazmin's husband starts clapping, which jolts our attention. "Hey! Enough with the games. So you're the guy who slept with my wife."

"You slept with his wife?" Diamond says.

Natasha looks at me. "You slept with his wife?"

"No! We went to some swingers club, but nothing happened."

"You invited my wife to a swingers club?" Jazmin's husband shouts.

"I didn't invite her. She invited me."

"Which swingers club?" Diamond asks.

"The one past Martin Luther King," I say.

"Ahh, that's a good one. Did you check out the pool?" Diamond says.

"Okay! Enough already!" Natasha yells. "I'm the one with the gun, so I'm calling the shots here. Where is his wallet?"

Diamond straightens up as if the Soviet Guard has spoken. She looks at the kitchen counter and there next to a big jar of pretzels is my wallet.

"Okay, irate husband, go over and bring it to me. Slowly!" Natasha commands.

The guy moves like a whisper. He's wearing brown Hush Puppies. Hey, I have the same shoes. This is weird. You can hear a pin drop in here. The guy grabs my wallet and holds it up. Now he really looks like me.

The window smashes! The Doberman lunges through, barking. I duck.

"Go get 'em, Max! Good boy!" Diamond yells.

The dog grabs the wallet as if it's a piece of meat, and then hops back through the window.

"My hand! That dog almost took my hand off!" Jazmin's husband screams.

Not another dog! I hate dogs! I had enough. I dive through the window and shout, "My I.D. badge!"

"My matchbook!" Natasha yells, riding my coattails.

"Get back here, you adulterer!" Jazmin's husband shouts at the door.

"Max, come back, boy!" Diamond says from the back of the pack.

I'm running through the yard. I clear the fence. The dog is galloping down the street. I can catch it; I know I can.

The dog runs past my car. Smokin' is putting a boot on my wheel and that chubby guy is removing my hubcaps.

"Hey! That's my car!" I yell.

Should I stop to protect my car or go after the dog? Which one? I can always get another car, but I can't get another I.D. badge. I pick up the pace.

Natasha, Jazmin's husband, and Diamond are following me. "Strip it all off!" Jazmin's husband says to Smokin' and that chubby guy.

The dog runs through the next intersection. It's damn fast. What can I do to stop it? "Want some more candy, boy?" I yell, but the dog keeps going.

Headlights are approaching at the cross street. I can't stop!

The horn blares. The compact car screeches to a stop. I go to jump over it, but hit the hood and roll off. Ouch!

Jazmin is inside driving. A figure is next to her in the passenger seat. It's Peaches!

"Hey, there's my love!" Peaches yells.

"There's my husband!" Jazmin shouts, looking at him running behind me.

Not Peaches! Now I have something to run away from. I look back and see Natasha flip in the air and clear the hood. She's good!

"Roger, honey, get that bastard!" Jazmin yells.

"My love, get back here!" Peaches shouts like James Earl Jones winning his Emmy Award. Now there's an overweight boxcar on the train of people following me.

I channel all of my rage, all of my energy, all of the oppression this city has caused me into my muscles. If I can get back my I.D., I can get back my life. I just want my life back!

The dog is still four houses in front of me. There's another cross street. Headlights from another car are coming.

This is the one time a car should hit an animal. It's a Ford Taurus with only one headlight. Is that Javier?

The car's brakes lock. The dog slows. It's an old gray-haired man. Where the hell is Javier when you need him? A bizarre memory surfaces in my brain—that house party on College Avenue. It was an October night just like this one, back in my senior year. It was the night that I discovered the penis on that blonde "chick." I ran out of that back bedroom and to my shower in ten minutes without stopping. And they were three miles apart!

A burst of energy traverses through my body. I'm closing in on the Doberman. What is motivating that dog to run? Things that dog could never comprehend motivate me.

The dog shakes its head. It must be getting tired. The condom in my wallet falls out. My foot crushes it, even though I try to avoid it. Then, the matchbook hits the street. Natasha will be happy.

"Max, get back here!" Diamond screams.

She must be way in the back. I never knew escorts could run.

The Doberman is slowing. "I got you, you dumb dog!" I yell.

Shadows consume the roadway. The macadam ends. Now I'm chasing the dog on a dirt path.

"Max! Stop! The cliff!" Diamond yells.

I'm six feet away from the dog. What is Diamond talking about? What does she mean by *the cliff*?

Then the dog hits the brakes, stopping dead. I lower down and grab my wallet from its mouth. While the dog only has seventy pounds to stop, I have one hundred and seventy.

My momentum keeps me going past the dog. It's now clear what Diamond means by *the cliff.*

I soar into the darkness. There's no ground left and I tumble down a mountain, over and over and over. My body bashes into the unyielding desert. Isn't the desert supposed to be flat? Just as everything else, this city is full of surprises. Bizarrely, this reminds me of my youth, rolling down the hill by my elementary school with my best friend, Tony. I haven't talked to Tony in ten years. Where is he right now? He's not running alongside of me, cheering me on as I roll down this hill. I'm all alone out here. Gone is the soft autumn grass, replaced by jagged rocks and dirt. This may be the last hill I roll down, the last thing I will ever do.

After two dozen tumbles, gravity gives up. I can't move. I can't see. I can't breathe. All I can do is lie here. Will someone come down to save me? How will they even get down?

My Big Wheel is under the Christmas tree. My dad and my mom are smiling. They're pointing at the Big Wheel. I want the Big Wheel. Then, there's black.

# 15

What are the names of those cream-filled Christmas trees? You know, those little layered cakes in the shape of Christmas trees with stripes of red icing and scattered green sprinkles. I haven't had one since I was a kid. They tasted so yummy. Mmm.

I'm walking down the stairs toward my kitchen. I'm in my house in Pennsylvania. It's warm and I'm wearing my pajamas. The lights are on in the kitchen. Sweet smells swirl in the air. Something's cooking.

There's my grandmother, my dad's mom, in the kitchen. She's making Christmas Eve dinner. There are her Slovakian dishes. Pierogies are cooking in melted butter. Fish is in the oven. And there's Grandma's famous cheese bread on the side of the stove.

Grandma smiles at me. Her eyes are warmer than a summer night in the Poconos. She has something in her hand. It's one of those cream-filled Christmas trees.

"Go on. I know they're your favorite, Benjamin. You can have one before dinner. I won't tell your mom."

"I love you, Grandma." I give her a hug and hold her tightly, getting lost in the serenity of Grandma. The last time I hugged her was on her deathbed five years ago.

I open the package and bite off the top stripe of red icing on the Christmas tree. Mmm. There it is. I offer Grandma a bite, but she smiles and shakes her head. She looks so happy.

"Can you help me get the fish out of the oven?" she asks.

I smile and put on the oven mitts near the stove. As I open the oven, there's no fish, only rocks and sand baking in a pan. It's so bright that I have to close my eyes. What the hell is going on?

I open my eyes. The desert is staring at me. The sun enters my pupils and stabs my brain. Where am I? It's so bright.

Grandma is standing over me, but her face is different. It's young, smooth, sexy. It's Natasha.

I'm lying at the base of a mountain. Natasha helps me sit up, my bones crying.

"What happened?" I ask her.

"This city ate you alive."

Two more people are at my side. Hey! It's Javier, handcuffed and clutched in the hands of that Russian guy from the van. Deep wrinkles are in the Russian's brow, wrinkles that must have been put there by the Cold War.

"Benjamin!" Javier shouts.

I rise up as fast as my beaten body lets me. My bones ache. Did I break anything? Everything's moving, just painfully. My black pants are torn on the right knee and my shirt is caked with dirt.

"What are you doing with him?" I say.

The angry Russian spouts off some foreign words.

"He says that Javier is lying about his real identity. He says that he is a computer hacker," Natasha translates.

"Benjamin, you have to tell them that I don't know anything about hacking. You know I only look up porn on that thing."

Javier is squirming. Fear coats his eyes. Part of me feels bad, yet another part of me feels that he's getting what he deserves. But just as two soldiers share a drink and two passing bikers share a wave, two college roommates share a bond that always exists. Although roommates come and go, the only true roommates are roommates in college.

"Yeah, Javier is telling the truth. I can vouch for him. You *are* telling the truth, right?"

"Benjamin. I'm sorry, man. All those times you asked me to be your wingman and then I just stiffed you. All those bummed dollars and times I forgot to close the refrigerator." Javier breaks down, tears flowing from his eyes.

"This is so pathetic," Natasha says.

I've never seen Javier cry before, but then again, I've never been to Vegas before either. Is there a way to go over there and upload all our memories together into that Russian's brain? Is there a way to uncuff my roommate, my friend? Although I can't speak Russian, I can speak geek.

"*I* did it," I announce.

Javier looks up. Natasha narrows her eyes. The wrinkles on the angry Russian's forehead deepen.

"I used a proxy to tunnel through Javier's computer to breach the computer network at the Russian Embassy."

"What are you talking about, Benjamin? Don't take the fall on this. I owe you so much. I'm so sorry, man," Javier says through tears.

Then I let go. Beyond those broken promises and I-owe-yous, all those years together were filled with laughs and memories that are so deeply a part of me. Without Javier there next to me during those stressful days at Penn State, I wouldn't be here today, a geek versus Vegas.

"I'm sorry, Javier," I say, tears pouring from my eyes.

"I love you, man," he says.

"I love you too," I reply.

"This is worse than reality TV," Natasha says.

Suddenly, the Happy Florist van slams to a stop at the top of the mountain. The side door opens and out comes two more Russians holding a man with a bag covering his head. Who the hell is that?

"Is that me?" I say.

One of the Russians yanks off the mask. It's Javier's Vegas roommate, the Grace Kelly lover. The Russians exchange some words with Natasha. Then they toss the roommate back inside the van and speed away.

"What's happening?" I say.

"The other guy confessed to it all, including using Javier's computer when he was not home. Plus they matched those other IP addresses to laptops found in his locked room and car. I guess you guys are off the hook."

The angry Russian uncuffs Javier. He runs over. Should I hug him? I don't want to look gay. I lean in right, but Javier leans into my right too. We back up, chuckle, and then shake hands.

Natasha pushes us together. "Just hug already!" she goes.

I give Javier a big hug, and he gives me an even bigger one.

"Let's, uh, never tell anyone we've, uh, hugged, okay?" he goes.

"I'll be sure to leave it out when I tell this story to my grandkids."

"They'll never believe you," he says.

"You're right."

The Russian guy starts talking to Natasha. The only word I make out is *vodka.*

Javier perks up and speaks some Russian. The angry Russian laughs and smiles, the wrinkles in his brow flattening.

"I never knew you spoke Russian," I say.

"Hey, even though I slept through Russian class at Penn State, I did learn how to say, *Let's have a vodka over a plate of bacon.*"

"That's random," I reply.

"I knew it would come in handy one day. See, a college education *is* worth it."

"So now you're friends with this guy?" I ask.

"Hey, it was all a misunderstanding, right?" he says. "Plus, these Russians love their booze. I can respect that."

"That we do," Natasha adds.

"Hey, Benjamin didn't tell me about you. Did you guys, uh…" Javier puts his pointer finger into the hole his other hand makes.

"No!" Natasha shouts as her Russian comrade laughs.

Part of me feels that this whole bizarre night, all of the running, dodging, and bonding was better than sex. Then another part of me shoots and kills this first part and says, "Hell no!"

"You take care, man. Let's keep in touch more. I'll come out to LA and buy you a drink, and then we can pull an all-nighter," he says.

"No more all-nighters," I reply.

He smiles, and then winks, nodding at Natasha, telling me to go for it without words.

The Russian guy and Javier share a handshake and some more Russian words. They both climb up the hill. Now it's just Natasha and me.

There's dried blood on my arms, nothing too bad. In front of me are ten stories of mountain.

"Wow, did I fall all that way?" I say.

Next to me are pieces of my cell phone and my wallet. Inside is my I.D. badge showing Benjamin Pollock, the Information Systems Policy Analyst at Pegman Telecommunications. He looks different, because there are two teeth marks covering his face. Do you think the dog liked the taste?

"Hurry up," Natasha says.

With my life back in my hands, she helps me climb.

Reaching the top is bittersweet—sweet in that I made it back to the streets of Vegas, and bitter in that I made it back to the streets of Vegas. I walk down the road with Natasha toward the sun. If I keep going, I'll be back in Pennsylvania by the time I'm thirty.

A kid is riding a bike and throwing newspapers. I lock eyes with him for a second. He knows exactly what happened to me.

We reach a cross street. Natasha stops walking. Could I go with her, leaving this life behind me? Natasha is the woman I've been looking for.

"I can't go any further with you," she says.

"But I could help you on your next mission. We could be a team. I could be a secret agent and—"

She puts her finger over my mouth, silencing me.

"I've never met anyone like you, Benjamin." She leans in, her scent swirling through my brain. She kisses my cheek, her lips electrifying my body, and sends a whisper into my ear, "Just be yourself."

"Will I ever see you again?" I ask.

All she does is smile, the morning sun catching the curve of her face, the warm desert air playing with her hair. This image burns permanently into my brain like a string of ones and zeros onto a hard drive. From this moment forward, no matter what happens to me in this crazy world, this image of beauty will be right there in my mind, hidden away from all the stresses in the world. She will always be with me.

Natasha turns to walk away, but then she stops and reaches under her dress. My heart stops as she tosses me a key.

"Is this the key to your heart?" I whisper.

"It's the key to *your* heart," she replies.

Then she walks toward the sun, letting it take her away.

What exactly is this key? After five minutes of stumbling down the road, I see my car, or at least, what's left of it. Ahh, this key. It unlocks the boot on my wheel.

My 2006 Scion xB used to look generic, so generic that people would often laugh at it, especially women. Now it's the opposite of generic. The rear window is blown out. Graffiti covers its brown paint. The hubcaps are missing, leaving black steel wheels. There are more dents than those on a retired Vegas stripper. The car is hurting, its pain and suffering oozing from its metal. It's been with me the whole night.

I click the keyless entry, but the car remains dead. I try the door, but it's locked. Wow, the handle is cold. Maybe it really is dead. But there is a way inside.

I roll through the rear window and crawl to the driver's seat. My stereo is missing. Is the engine still there? I put the key into the ignition and turn it. The engine cranks, and then finally starts.

"Thank you," I say.

As I pull out, Diamond's house calls to me. The blinds are open in the front window. Jazmin, her husband, Peaches, Diamond, Smokin', and that chubby guy are eating breakfast and sharing laughs. But there's one person in particular missing—one person who made this crazy night worth it.

I find my way out of the suburban mess and drive past the Strip. The lights on the casinos are not lit. The buildings look inferior under the sun. No longer are they enticing and mesmerizing. They are just buildings without lights.

This city is so bizarre. It really is the city of sin lost in the desert. Millions of people come here every year, drawn to the girls, the booze, the gambling, the sex, but once those lights go out, all you have is yourself. Vegas can only satisfy an artificial need. You think the city can solve your problems, but it can't—only *you* can solve your problems. Eventually those millions of people realize a singular truth, just as I have: *the house always wins*.

Passing the back of the Vegas sign, I read the warning aloud, "Drive Carefully – Come Back Soon." The biggest word on the sign is the word *carefully*, yet people still don't get it.

# 16

After two hours of driving, my head is pounding. I need to sleep for a week. I pull over in Barstow. At least I don't have to lie about calling in sick. I'm beyond sick. There's a payphone outside a gas station.

I leave the door open when I park. A drifter with a grizzly beard is sitting on a concrete stoop, drinking from a paper bag.

"Do you have the time?" I ask him.

He gestures to a large clock on top of a bank. "Ten after eight."

My pockets are empty. I check the coin return on the phone and feel the cold metal. Maybe I have some quarters in my glove box. Were there any in there when I was rooting around earlier? Nah, I don't think so.

The drifter reads my mind. He stands up and tosses me two coins. “There’re two quarters to rub together. You probably need ’em more than me,” he says, walking off.

I dial the number that is still ingrained in my mind. You’d think I would have forgotten it with all the new information squeezed into my skull.

It rings, and then I hear the voice of one of our secretaries. They all sound the same. “Pegman Telecom. How may I help you?”

“Dipple,” I say.

“*Dipple*? Oh, silly. You forgot the title. I’ll page her.”

There’s a penis drawn on the phone with a pen. Does this have to be right in front of my face? On the side of the parking lot, two dogs are mating. Really? I look back at the penis.

“This is Ms. Dipple.” The voice of the stresses in my life enters my ear and tries to control my brain, but my brain is already dead.

“This is Benjamin calling.”

“Benjamin, where are you? You’re already ten minutes late.”

Should I tell her how a guy in an abandoned warehouse nearly shot me, how a morbidly obese woman at a swingers club almost squeezed me to death, how a hooker hooked me with her scam, and how Russian spies almost killed my roommate and me? My head starts throbbing. “I’m not feeling well today.”

“Not feeling well! That’s unacceptable!”

Her words intensify the ache in my head. A car honks its horn behind me. I’m ready to hang up and drive the other way, not stopping until I reach Pennsylvania.

"What's that noise? Where are you?"

"That's the TV. I'm, uh, going to take a sick day."

"No, you're not. I have a very important task for you today."

She's going to fire me. I had a feeling about this yesterday. "Can't you just let Bob do the task? I can't explain the intense pain I feel at the moment."

"I have Bob doing the J.R.S. reports. I don't care if you lopped off your leg, you are coming in today."

"But—"

"If you don't, you can kiss your job goodbye, buster."

I look at the graffiti on my car. All along, it appeared to be just random lines of colors, but there's a shape there—the shape of a chicken.

"What's your decision?" Ms. Dipple says.

My voice wants to tell her to shove it, to go to hell in a hurry, but my brain thinks back to my logic class at Penn State. In that class, the professor said that logic could be applied to all equations in life. If A is greater than B, and B is greater than C, then logic tells us that A is greater than C. Logic trumps emotion, trumps pain, trumps stress. Logic is logic. If the sun goes down at night, then it will rise in the morning, no matter what happens during the night.

Although I want to quit this job and move back home, I need to do it without haste and using logic.

"Okay," I say. "But I won't be in for at least two hours."

"Get here A.S.A.P."

And then I hang up the phone.

After driving back to the concrete jungle and parking in my garage, a roach greets me on the ground. He's about an inch in length, the kind that they used to eat on *Fear Factor*. Normally, insects terrify me, especially roaches, but this little guy seems as if he knows me. Has he been waiting for me to park in my parking space?

As I step out, the roach stays still. He's alive because his tiny tentacles are moving, assessing my movements. Could I pick up this roach and put him in my pocket? Could he come upstairs and talk to Ms. Dipple? Could he live with me? But my apartment complex doesn't allow pets. The roach comes over and touches my dusty shoes, dust from the Mojave Desert. He understands what has happened; he understands me.

"Thank you," I say, and then the roach scurries away on the dank concrete.

I'm standing in the elevator with my reflection in the stainless steel. My shirt is torn and the white has become dusty brown. My black pants look like they're from an '80s rock band. Although the metal distorts my face, spots of dried blood are painting it. Then there's the one thing that I fought for all night—my I.D. badge hanging from my neck.

The elevator opens on my floor, and then I'm back at work. Have I been gone a year? Maybe I have.

"The dead walks," Gary says.

I walk past Regina, the former hooker. She doesn't call me *cutie patootie* or *lover boy*. She says nothing when I pass—a first.

I almost make it to my cubicle when Bob sees me. "Hey, where've you been? Man, what the hell happened to you?"

"Don't ask."

"Hey, Ms. Dipple has been looking for you."

"There he is," Ms. Dipple says from behind me. Her mouth drops when I turn around. "Oh my God. What kind of disease do you have?"

"I'm here," I say.

"I know Mr. Pegman relaxed the dress code policy, but *this*? We give you a foot and you take a mile," she says.

"It's an inch," I reply.

"What?"

"It's we give you an *inch* and you take a mile," I clarify.

"Well, an inch and a foot are both a measure of distance."

"That's true, but you can't change an idiom. Unless you're Biff Tannen."

Bob smiles and gives me a nod.

"Well, anyway," she says. "I'm glad you made it in. I need you to train our new hire."

So this is the reason that she made me come in, the reason that I can't get sleep. Doesn't she have any compassion?

"New hire?" I say. "Can't wait to see what retirement home you recruited him from."

"It's a she."

Ms. Dipple gestures toward the empty cubicle, but now it's not empty. A woman is sitting at the desk. She's not middle-aged, elderly, over-the-hill, beyond her years. She's a young woman with a petite figure, long brown hair, and stylish black-framed glasses.

"This is Stacy. She just moved here from Ohio," Ms. Dipple says.

She stands up and offers me her hand with a smile—a smile that I've never seen in this office, in this city, or in the West.

"It's Pennsylvania, ma'am. I just graduated from Penn State."

Wait. What did she say?

"This is Benjamin. He's one of Pegman Telecom's best Information Systems Policy Analysts…when he wants to be." She adds her little Dipple laugh. Then she looks at me. "I need you to run her through all the updated policies we've been creating, especially the I.D. badge. The new PR campaign is in full force." She looks at the teeth marks on my badge. "Hey, what happened to yours?"

"Ms. Dipple, Mr. Pegman would like to see you," one of the front-office secretaries says.

"Okay, have at it," Ms. Dipple says to Stacy and me.

Bob winks at me and goes back to his cubicle.

"I didn't know that dust and torn clothes were part of the dress code," Stacy says.

"It's a very, very long story," I say, brushing off some of the dust.

She chuckles and asks, "Is that your cubicle?"

Everything on my desk is just as I left it. "Yeah, it looks like we have something in common." I point at the blue and white poster.

"Get out! I'll never forget Penn State and my room-mates," Stacy says, pointing at a picture on her desk, a picture that wasn't there yesterday. It shows Stacy standing with a red cup between two other girls, one Asian and the other Hispanic. They're all smiling.

I grab my chair and slide it over to her desk.

Bob returns. "Hey, Benjamin, you got a call. Some guy named Javier from Vegas. Says your cell phone isn't on. He wants to know how you made out with the Russian. It sounds like a crank call."

Javier and I have so much in common and we've shared so many years of our lives together. Javier knows things about me that no one knows, and I know things about him that everyone knows. However, there's one thing that we don't share, one thing that we will never share—he never took a logic class.

"Tell him I'm busy now, but all of my problems seem to be sorted out."

I grab some charts that I've been working on and show them to Stacy. "Here, let me give you the rundown of what we do. We draft new policies that affect everyone who touches an information system, which is everyone in here. Oh, by the way, do you like Happy Meals?"

"I love Happy Meals, especially the toy," she laughs.

"Well, I'm sure you'll get a great collection from working here." I gesture to my race car collection.

She leans in and whispers, "Seems that there are a lot of older people here, or is it just me?"

"Finally, someone else noticed."

"So who is Javier from Vegas? I've never been to Vegas. I'd love to take a road trip."

I hold my breath. Something tickles me inside my pants.

"Excuse me one second," I say.

"Sure."

If you told me yesterday that a young woman my age and from my college would be sitting next to me in the morning, I would've called you crazy. I thought getting laid would solve all of my problems, but all trying to get laid did was cloud my judgment and create new problems.

I stand up and walk to the bathroom, the urge to pee overwhelming. I'm not tired anymore. I'm not hungry or hurt. My headache is gone. I feel okay. Did last night even happen? Maybe it didn't. Maybe it was all a dream, like in those movies where the guy wakes up at the end. Either way, I have learned something since yesterday, something that a beautiful Russian woman told me, something that my grandmother always used to say.

That dog is walking around the floor. It looks at me and then goes the other way. I chuckle as I open the door to the bathroom. Inside, there's a utility worker dressed in white. He grabs a trowel of plaster and swipes it over the tile in front of the urinal. After he steps away, I walk over and start to pee. Ahh. Finally. Relief. Where's the crack? It's gone. There's only a perfect tile.

## About the Author:

Jonathan Sturak grew up in the Pocono Mountains of Pennsylvania. He is a Penn State University graduate and holds degrees in Computer Science and Film. He currently lives in Las Vegas where he uses the energy of the city to craft stories about life and the human condition. *The Place Called Home*, Sturak's essay about Eastern European heritage in Northeast Pennsylvania, was featured on *Glass Cases*, associate literary agent Sarah LaPolla's pop culture blog. Sturak is also a managing editor at NoirNation.com, the premier location for international crime fiction. His debut thriller novel *Clouded Rainbow* was published in December 2009 and has over 100,000 downloads on the Amazon Kindle. Sturak keeps updated information on his website at sturak.com

CPSIA information can be obtained at www.ICGtesting.com
Printed in the USA
LVOW13s0026190414

382284LV00001B/58/P